This is my Book
from

HE FELL BACKWARD UPON THE LITTLE STERN DECK.

"Buddy and the G-Man Mystery" (See Page 128)

Buddy and the G-Man Mystery

or

A Boy and a Strange Cipher

BY

HOWARD R. GARIS

Author of "Buddy Books," "Curlytops Books," "Teddy Books," Etc.

ILLUSTRATED

NEW YORK

CUPPLES & LEON COMPANY

THE BUDDY BOOKS

By HOWARD R. GARIS

12 mo. Cloth. Illustrated

BUDDY ON THE FARM
Or, A Boy and His Prize Pumpkin
BUDDY IN SCHOOL
Or, A Boy and His Dog
BUDDY AND HIS WINTER FUN
Or, A Boy in a Snow Camp
BUDDY AT RAINBOW LAKE
Or, A Boy and His Boat
BUDDY AND HIS CHUM
Or, A Boy's Queer Search
BUDDY AT PINE BEACH
Or, A Boy on the Ocean
BUDDY AND HIS FLYING BALLOON
Or, A Boy's Mysterious Airship
BUDDY ON MYSTERY MOUNTAIN
Or, A Boy's Strange Discovery
BUDDY ON FLOATING ISLAND
Or, A Boy's Wonderful Secret
BUDDY AND HIS SECRET CAVE
Or, A Boy and the Crystal Hermit
BUDDY AND HIS COWBOY PAL
Or, A Boy on a Ranch
BUDDY AND THE INDIAN CHIEF
Or, A Boy Among the Navajos
BUDDY AND THE ARROW CLUB
Or, A Boy and the Long Bow
BUDDY AT LOST RIVER
Or, A Boy and a Gold Mine
BUDDY ON THE TRAIL
Or, A Boy Among the Gypsies
BUDDY AT DEEP VALLEY
Or, A Boy on a Bee Farm
BUDDY AT RED GATE
Or, A Boy on a Chicken Farm
BUDDY IN DRAGON SWAMP
Or, A Boy on a Strange Hunt
BUDDY'S VICTORY CLUB
Or, A Boy and a Salvage Campaign
BUDDY AND THE G-MAN MYSTERY
Or, A Boy and a Strange Cipher

CUPPLES & LEON COMPANY, NEW YORK

Buddy and the G-Man Mystery

Printed in the U. S. A.

CONTENTS

BUDDY AND THE G-MAN MYSTERY

CHAPTER I

FLASHING SIGNALS

IT WAS a dark and stormy night. The rain dashed against the windows of the home of Richard (Buddy) Martyne as if it might break the glass. The wind moaned mournfully down the broad chimney of the living room fireplace.

No blaze crackled up the chimney, for it was late in June and the weather was warm. A hearth fire would have been out of place.

Mrs. Martyne, Buddy's mother, sat on one side of a table on which glowed a lamp. On the other side of the table sat Mr. Clayton Martyne, Buddy's father.

The red-haired boy himself was sprawled on

an easy chair in a corner of the room. Suddenly he sat up and said:

"Aw, gee whizz!"

"What's the matter?" asked Buddy's mother, looking up from her book.

"Sounds as if Buddy didn't like something," commented Mr. Martyne. He glanced up from some papers on which he was jotting down figures and smiled at his son.

"I don't like this rain!" exclaimed the red-haired boy.

"I'm afraid there isn't much you can do about it," his father remarked. "I never knew you to mind the rain before, Buddy. Seems to me I heard you mention that it rained several times when you were hunting the big lizards in Dragon Swamp."

"It did," agreed Buddy as he walked over to a window and flattened his nose against the glass. The rain dashed at his face harder than before, but Buddy stared out at it as if he could thus bring it to a stop. But it rained on.

"I didn't mind the rain then," went on Buddy, turning back toward his parents. "We were out in it and it was fun."

"And I suppose it was fun going out in the rain when you and your Victory Club were salvaging tin cans for the war effort," suggested Mrs. Martyne with a smile.

"Yes, it was," Buddy admitted. "But this rain comes at the wrong time. Tom Gordon and Harry Clee were coming over here tonight. We were going to plan what we could do this vacation. Now they won't come on account of the rain, I s'pose. But I'd like to know for sure whether they are coming or not. Can't I use the telephone?"

"No," answered Mr. Martyne. "The government and the telephone company has asked everybody not to use their telephones for unimportant messages. They might tie up the lines just when somebody else might want to use them for important war news."

"Oh, of course I don't want to go against the

government." Buddy was quick to say. "But I would like to telephone Tom and Harry."

"That isn't important," said Mr. Martyne. "If your boy friends don't come out in the rain tonight, you will probably see them tomorrow. Then you can settle about vacation plans."

"Maybe Tom and Harry will come out anyhow," suggested Buddy's mother. "They don't seem to me to be the sort of boys who would mind getting wet."

"No, they don't care about an ordinary storm," Buddy said. "But this is a fierce one. Have you and Dad made any plans about taking a vacation trip this year?" asked Buddy.

"No," answered his father. "The government has asked everyone to limit their pleasure travel this year. Gasolene is still scarce, and every civilian who travels on a railroad train, when he doesn't really need to, may keep a soldier or a sailor out of travel space. We are going to stay home this year, Buddy."

"Oh, well, I don't mind that—so much," said the red-haired boy. "Tom and Harry and I can probably have some fun. But I'd like to know what we can do. We were going to talk it over tonight. But with this storm, and not being able to use the telephone—"

"I thought you Boy Scouts could signal each other by flags," said Mrs. Martyne.

"We can," Buddy said. "That is when we are able to see one another. But I can't see either Tom or Harry now. And unless they knew I wanted to signal them they wouldn't be watching. You can't use signal flags after dark."

"How about flashlights?" asked his mother.

"Yes, we could use those if we had arranged it before hand," Buddy admitted. "I know the Morse code by flash lights and so do Tom and Harry. But they'd have to know I wanted to flash them some signals."

"Yes, I suppose it would need to be arranged in advance," admitted Mrs. Martyne.

"Well, you'd better prepare for that, Buddy. We are likely to have storms any time, now that Summer is at hand."

"That's right," Buddy agreed. "Gee whizz! Listen to that rain! And the wind! I guess Tom and Harry won't come out in this. To-morrow we'll get up some kind of a signal system. I can see Tom's house from our attic windows and Tom can see Harry's. We'll plan to send signals that way. It will be fun and something to do this Summer. We can signal by flags in daytime and by flashlights at night."

Buddy was walking back to the window again, to look out into the storm, when the door bell rang.

"Maybe that's Tom and Harry now!" shouted the red-haired lad as he dashed toward the hall. A moment later his parents heard him greeting his chums.

"I didn't think you'd come out in this storm," said Buddy.

"Oh, it isn't so bad," said Harry.

"Not with rubber boots and a rain coat," added Tom. "Say," he went on, "we'd better not come in any farther, Buddy, until we let some of this water dribble off us."

"That's right," said Harry. "We'll stand here in the vestibule until the rain runs off our coats."

"And if we could take off our boots here," said Tom, "we wouldn't get your mother's rugs all mud."

"I'll get you some of my old slippers," offered Buddy. He dashed up stairs while his chums waited in the tiled vestibule.

"Is it much of a storm, boys?" called Mr. Martyne.

"Fierce!" exclaimed Tom and Harry.

"Buddy was trying to think of some way of finding out whether or not you would venture into the storm," said Mrs. Martyne. "We didn't want him to use the telephone."

"My folks wouldn't let me use ours, either," spoke Tom.

"Same here," echoed Harry.

"That's why we should have some sort of a signal code," declared Buddy as he came sliding down the banister with two pairs of slippers for his guests. "We'll arrange for one now. I can see your attic windows from ours, Tom, and you can see Harry's from your house. So I can wig-wag you a message, Tom and you can flag Harry. Then he can wig-wag back to you and you can signal me. How about it?"

"Sounds good," declared Tom.

"Flags by day and lights by night," added Harry.

"'One if by land and two if by sea, and I on the opposite shore will be', like Paul Revere," said Buddy with a laugh. "Come on up to my room and we'll plan a signal code that we can use the next rainy night," he went on.

The three chums were soon in conference. They decided that, next day, they would try the flag-signalling system and at night try morning, Tom. I'll send you a message and you can relay it to Harry and then talk back to me."

"Sure!" echoed the two.

The plan worked perfectly. With his Boy Scout signal flags next morning, Buddy sent this message to Tom:

"Ask Harry if he will come over to my house this afternoon?"

In a short time Tom signalled back to Buddy:

"Message received. Harry and I will be there."

That afternoon, talking over their signal success at Buddy's home, the boys planned to send flashing signals that night.

So at 9 P. M. Buddy, with his flashlight, took his place in his attic window. He had hardly signalled to Tom, getting back an acknowledgment that the fire sirens began to wail.

"Air raid alarm," Buddy flashed to Tom.

"Yes, I heard it," Tom signalled back in

sending each other messages by means of dots and dashes, in the Morse Code, with small flashlights.

With this to interest them, the three boys soon forgot all about the rain. Though they did not realize it, the plans they made that night were to have an effect on a strange mystery which might have had disastrous results on the war effort, except for what Buddy and his chums were able to do.

But now the thoughts of the boys were not on war. After arranging for sending signals next day from the attic windows of their homes, they talked of the recent success of Buddy's Victory Club, and discussed some of the exciting times the red-haired boy had experienced in Dragon Swamp.

When Tom and Harry went to their homes that night the storm was about over.

"It'll be a good day for signalling by flags tomorrow," Buddy told his chums. "Be in your attic window at 9 o'clock sharp tomorrow

Morse Code. "I'll ask Harry if he heard it."

Buddy waited, meanwhile sending out practice words in Morse but not directing his flashlight toward Tom's windows. Tom had gone to another window of his attic to signal Harry.

In the midst of his signal flashes Buddy heard a violent ringing of the doorbell of his house.

CHAPTER II

A WARNING

Buddy listened for a moment to make sure his father or mother would answer the persistent ringing of the front door bell. He heard his father's steps in the lower hall. Then the red-haired boy prepared to resume his practice signal flashing from his attic window to that of Tom Gordon.

"I guess maybe," said Buddy to himself, as he flickered his little torch, "that's somebody asking dad to go out on air raid warden work. Maybe the man who has our sector in charge couldn't get out." He heard his father's voice at the front door. Also another voice—an excited voice. Buddy had walked part way from the room, to look down the stairs. He noted that the house was in darkness because of the black-out rule in a simulated air raid.

He now walked back and took his place by

the window again to flash this message to Tom:

"Any air raid excitement over your way?"

Buddy had spelled out, in dot and dash Morse letters, the first two words of his message when he heard feet coming rapidly up the attic stairs. And a strange voice shouted:

"Stop that signalling? Who are you? Don't you know there's an air raid test going on?"

Buddy was so surprised he didn't know what to answer. He cut the switch of his small flashlight and waited in the darkness. The footsteps came into the room. Then a dim blue light showed and a voice said:

"I'm Mr. Blake—the air raid warden for this street. Who are you and why are you signalling in the black-out?"

"I—why—I'm Buddy Martyne," was the red-haired boy's answer. "I am sending signals to my chum Tom Gordon. I—I guess I forgot all about the black-out, Mr. Blake."

"Buddy, I'm surprised at you," came the voice of his father. Mr. Martyne was ascending the attic stairs. He, also, carried a dim blue flashlight, the gleam of which could not have been seen if there had been hostile planes in the sky.

"Gee, Dad, I'm sorry!" said Buddy, contritely.

"I had no idea you were signalling," went on Mr. Martyne. "When Mr. Blake rang our bell and said a report had been made that strange signals were flashing from our attic windows I hardly believed him. But we went outside and looked. We saw the flashes."

"Yes—yes, they were mine," said Buddy in a low voice. "There's Tom signalling now. I guess he wants to know what's wrong."

"Well, as long as it is only you boys," said Mr. Blake in kinder tones, "I won't report you to the Civilian Defense office. But please signal Tom to stop his flashes."

"I will," said Buddy. "Shall I tell him to signal Harry to cut his out, too?"

"You had better," advised Mr. Martyne.

Out into the darkness went Buddy's signals. Then, after a pause, Tom flashed a message to Harry, though Buddy could not see it.

"I'm sorry about this, Mr. Blake," apologized Mr. Martyne as the three went down stairs in the dim blue illumination.

"Oh, there's no great harm done," said the warden. "Of course if there had been a real air raid, the flashing signals that Buddy and his chums sent out from their attic windows might have guided enemy planes over Mountchester. But this was only a test to keep us on the alert. I'm sure Buddy won't do it again."

"I certainly will not!" exclaimed Buddy. "And Tom and Harry won't, either. I'll tell them."

"I think other air raid wardens have already warned your chums," said Mr. Blake as he went out the front door. His white metal helmet gleamed faintly in the blue light from Mr. Martyne's dim-out torch.

"Gosh!" murmured Buddy as he and his

father went into the darkened living room, "I never thought this would happen!"

"I suppose, Buddy," spoke Mr. Martyne, "that many persons in countries that are now under the heel of the Nazis, are saying the same thing. We can't be too careful."

"That's right," Buddy agreed. "Then I suppose this is the end of any night signals for Tom, Harry and me."

"Night signals—yes," said Mrs. Martyne. "But you can use flags by day."

"Yes, and have everybody reading our messages," objected Buddy. "We wanted to have something secret."

"It wasn't very secret, flashing lights from attic windows," said Mr. Martyne.

"Oh, not so many in Mountchester can read Morse," spoke Buddy. "What Tom, Harry and I flashed wasn't known to very many. But we won't do it at night any more."

"If you boys want to have real secret communications," said Mrs. Martyne, "why don't you get up a code or cipher?"

"What's that?" Buddy asked.

"Well," said his mother, "when we get the all-clear signal I'll tell you."

"Do you mean," asked the red-haired boy, "that Tom and Harry and I can send messages, openly, that nobody else can read?"

"I wouldn't say no one else could read them," spoke Mrs. Martyne as she sat in the darkened room, waiting for the all-clear signal. "For nearly every cipher or code that has been used has also been solved. The various governments of the world are always trying to read the codes and ciphers of the other governments, especially in war time. But some codes and ciphers are very difficult to read except by those in the secret who have the key."

"What's the difference between a code and a cipher?" asked Buddy. He was beginning to be much interested.

"A code," explained his mother, "and I happen to know, Buddy, because I have been reading a book about secret communications, a code is a set of words, usually short words.

"Each word stands for some other word or a set of words or a phrase. Take the word 'plum.' It could mean something like: 'We have met the enemy and they are ours.' That would be a fine plum. The person who sent the message, by wireless, by flashlight or by wig-wag flags, would have a book in which appeared all the code words. The person to whom the message was sent would have a similar book.

"So, when he received the word 'plum' he could look it up in his book and know there had been a victory. Only the persons having use of the code books would know the meaning of the message."

"I would think," said Buddy, "that these code books could be stolen, and then the enemy could intercept messages."

"That often happens," said Mrs. Martyne. "For that reason the codes are often changed. And in the Navy, which makes use of many code messages, the code books are always bound in lead covers. Thus if there is likelihood of the vessel being captured, an officer throws the code book overboard and it sinks. The enemy can't use it."

"Golly. I'd like to be in the navy!" exclaimed Buddy. "I think Tom and Harry and I will get up a code. Then we can send messages nobody can understand even if they spell out the words we send."

"Yes, you can do that," agreed his mother. "But getting up a code isn't easy. And you would always need the code book with you unless you used only a few code words and memorized them. But you might use a cipher."

"What's a cipher?" Buddy wanted to know.

Before his mother could answer, the all-clear sounded. And as Mrs. Martyne had some housework to do, which was interrupted by the air raid warning, she told Buddy she would explain about ciphers some other time.

"Say, this is going to be interesting!" exclaimed Buddy as he jumped up in the air and clicked his heels together three times. This was a trick his uncle had taught him. "I'm going to call up Tom and Harry and tell them we're going to send messages after this in cipher."

Buddy started for the telephone, but his father said:

"No wire messages, son. The ban is still on. You'll see your chums in the morning."

"All right," Buddy agreed.

Tom and Harry were over at Buddy's house early next day. They seemed angry about something as Buddy could tell by their faces.

"What's wrong?" he asked.

"Aw, my sister knows all about it," said Tom.

"So does mine!" added Harry.

"All about what?" asked Buddy, somewhat puzzled.

"Those messages we sent last night before

the air raid wardens stopped us," explained Tom. "I guess we should have known better, but I sort of forgot about the black-out."

"Yes," agreed Buddy, "we pulled a boner there. But how did Lucy and Mary find out about the messages?"

"They were spying on us," said Tom. "At least my sister was."

"And so was Mary," added Harry, referring to his sister. "They were over at Agnes Reynolds's house and from there, up in the top story, they can see the attic windows of all our houses. So they saw the signals and—"

"Quiet!" warned Tom. "Here they come now."

As he spoke, Lucy Gordon, Mary Clee and Agnes Reynolds, the latter being Buddy's cousin, came walking along the street in front of Buddy's house. They were laughing and giggling.

"Secret and confidential," said Agnes, mockingly.

"Meet me down at the fish shack in the river," spoke Lucy.

"And bring worms for bait," added Mary.

"Why—why!" exclaimed Buddy. "Those are some of the messages we flashed last night."

"I told you they spied," said Tom, gloomily.

"How could you read our signals?" asked Buddy.

"Oh," said his cousin lightly. "We are Girl Scouts. We know the Morse code."

"No use keeping anything from girls," declared Harry in tragic tones.

"We'll read every message you send!" boasted Lucy.

"Will you? Well, I guess you won't!" declared Buddy. "From now on our messages are going to be in code or cipher. Come on down to the fish shack, fellows, and I'll explain."

CHAPTER III

CODES AND CIPHERS

THE fish shack, toward which Buddy and his chums were now hurrying, was a sort of clubhouse on the river. It was on some land Mr. Martyne owned and Buddy had the use of it. There was a dock, some row boats and a small sail boat. Some day Buddy hoped to have a boat with at least an outboard motor.

The three chums used to meet at the shack and start out on fishing trips. They also held impromptu meetings there. But the shack had not been in use much since the previous Summer. Then Buddy and his chums had fitted up a clubhouse in half of the Martyne garage. From there the tin can salvage campaign was carried on as told in the book just before this one, "Buddy and the Victory Club."

The old fish shack, however, was often a meeting place for Buddy, Tom, Harry and other Mountchester boys. It could not be used in Winter for it wasn't heated. But now that Summer had come again, Buddy and his friends planned to have fun with the fish shack as a starting point.

"What's all this about codes and ciphers?" asked Tom as the three entered the shack and went out on the float in front.

"And how are we going to keep the girls from intercepting our messages?" inquired Harry.

"I don't know, but my mother does," answered Buddy.

"Is your mother coming down here?" asked Tom.

"No, but we'll be going up to my house soon," replied the red-haired boy. "I wanted to come down here where we could talk without those girls hearing us."

"Oh, secrets, eh?" asked Tom.

"And we have to put 'em down in codes and

ciphers—whatever they are—is that it?" asked Harry.

"Sort of," said Buddy. "But first, have you fellows heard anything about the National Electric Factory?"

"You mean it's closed down?" asked Tom.

"No," said Buddy, "it's working over time. But I heard my father telling Mr. Tort, the grocer, that a lot of shipments lately had been damaged by sabotage. You know the factory is turning out war goods. So maybe there are some spies or saboteurs around here."

"Maybe there are," said Tom. "The F.B.I. men got some during our tin can salvage drive. But there may be more. What's that got to do with codes and ciphers, Buddy."

"Yes; do a bit of de-coding," invited Harry.

"I will," promised the red-haired boy.

Buddy took from his pocket several slips of paper. From the glimpses Tom and Harry managed to get, the papers appeared to be covered with a jumble of letters and figures.

"This a cipher," said Buddy, picking out one paper.

"A cipher is a zero, and zero is nothing," chuckled Tom.

"I'm about as wise as I was before," spoke Harry.

"I'll explain, or, maybe, my mother had better do it," said Buddy. "She gave me the idea after we discovered the girls could read our dot and dash flashlight signals."

"Can we fool the girls?" asked Tom.

"And how!" exclaimed Buddy. "Wait until you hear about it. We can use a grille or a jargon."

"That last wouldn't be a golf club, by any chance, would it?" asked Harry, who was sometimes sarcastic.

"No," said Buddy. "They're both ciphers. My mother knows more about it than I do. But maybe if we can fool the girls we can fool the saboteurs that are wrecking some of the work at the National Electric Co. That would be something to help along the war here, wouldn't it?"

"If there are saboteurs," agreed Tom.

"That's what we've got to find out," said Buddy. "Just as we had to find out who was putting a crimp in our salvage campaign. Now if you fellows are interested in codes and ciphers, come on up to my house and I'll get mother to explain."

"Gosh, this sounds interesting," said Harry.

"Is it anything like writing with secret, invisible ink?" asked Tom.

"Something like," said Buddy. "But we don't need invisible ink for us to send messages to each other. We can write one, give it to anybody and they can't make head or tail of it."

"Why not?" Harry asked.

"Because it's in a code or cipher," answered the red-haired lad. "I think we'll use a cipher, because, if we use a code, we'll have to carry around with us a code book with a lot of words in it."

"What will we need to carry if we use a cipher?" asked Tom.

"Just a grille or maybe a stick?" replied Buddy.

"What's a grille?" asked Tom.

"What kind of a stick?" was Harry's question.

"Oh, just a stick—like a piece of fish pole," Buddy said. "But a grille is more complicated. Come on—let's go up to my house and my mother will explain."

As the boys left the fish shack, Tom suddenly uttered a warning hiss. His chums glanced at him and Tom said:

"Here come the girls!"

"Always sneaking around!" complained Buddy as he saw his cousin, Agnes Randall, with Lucy Gordon and Mary Clee strolling down toward the shack.

"They couldn't have heard what we said," remarked Tom.

"If they did, it won't do them any good," said Buddy. "We're going to have a secret cipher that they couldn't read in a thousand years, even if they find it, unless we give them the clue of the grille or the stick."

"I'll never give 'em that," said Tom.

"Nor I," added Harry.

"Then we're all set," spoke Buddy. "Come on."

As the boys left the shack they met the smiling girls.

"Going fishing?" asked Mary.

"No," said her brother Harry, just a little shortly. "We've been fishing."

"You didn't catch much," remarked Lucy.

"Oh, yes we did," said her brother Tom.

"What?" asked Buddy's cousin Agnes. "I don't see any fish."

"We've caught a secret," said Buddy. "It's

one you girls will never find out, either!" he said somewhat angrily.

"Oh, won't we?" mocked his cousin. "Well, we read your flashlight signals all right, didn't we?"

"But you won't read our secret cipher!" boasted Buddy.

The three boys saw the three girls exchange surprised looks. Here was something new—a secret. All girls love secrets.

"We'll find out!" boasted Agnes as she and her two chums strolled on.

"When you do—tell us," said Tom.

"We—we defy you!" called Harry.

The girls laughed.

"After all," said Buddy, as he and his chums walked on up to his house, "maybe we could let them in on the cipher business."

"Never!" said Tom.

"Never!" echoed Harry.

"But they saved us from the locked ice box," said Buddy, referring to what had happened as told in the book "Buddy and the Victory Club."

"If the girls are going to be in on this cipher secret, then count me out!" exclaimed Tom.

"Same here!" said Harry.

CHAPTER IV

STICK AND STRIP

BUDDY Martyne looked sharply at his two chums. Then the red-haired boy leaped into the air and clicked his heels together three times before he descended. None of Buddy's chums could do this trick. Tom and Harry looked at Buddy admiringly and Tom asked:

"What does that mean?"

"It means," answered Buddy, with a smile, "that if you fellows don't want the girls in on our new code and cipher secret they aren't going to be in. I'm with you on this."

"The three secret cipherers!" laughed Tom.

"One for all and all for one," quoted Harry.

"Now come on up to our house," Buddy went on, "and I'll ask my mother to explain about codes and ciphers."

As the three walked away together, they

looked back and saw the three girls approaching the fish shack.

"Looks as if they were going in," remarked Tom.

"What if they do?" asked Buddy. "There's nothing they can find out. We haven't left any code books there."

"Anyhow, the girls sort of have a right to go to the shack," spoke Harry. "They belong to the Victory Club and we used to hold meetings in the shack."

"That's right," chimed in Buddy. "The girls can go to the shack as often as they please. But they won't intercept any more of our secret messages. From now on we communicate by means of a code or cipher. I guess it will be a cipher as we don't want to make up a code book."

"Besides, the girls might find one of the books and then they'd know as much as we do," suggested Tom.

"Right!" exclaimed Harry.

"But what's the idea of all this cipher business, Buddy?" asked Tom. "We used to signal each other with flags by day and flashlights at night."

"The night signals are out from now, on account of the air raids precautions," said Buddy. "But we might want to send messages to each other, by night or day, and with a cipher we can do this right under the noses of the girls and they'll never know a thing about it."

"Must be something mysterious about a cipher," said Tom.

"There is," said Buddy. "Wait until you hear mother tell about Lysander of Sparta."

"Who was he?" Harry inquired.

"He was the king or commander or somebody who crushed the Athenian Empire in the sea fight at Aegospotami, captured that city and went on to the Hellespont."

"I don't know all that stuff you're rattling off, Buddy," said Tom, "but I remember the

Hellespont. It's the strait that connects the Aegean with the Sea of Marmora."

"And Lord Byron swam it," added Harry.

"And it's going to figure a lot in this war we're having," went on Buddy.

"You aren't thinking of getting us in this war; are you?" asked Tom. "We're too young, but we'll do our part in the salvage campaign and war stamp sales and the like of that."

"This code and cipher secret we're going to learn," said Buddy, with something of an air of mystery, "may have something to do with war. I mean we may get a chance to use a cipher in helping some G men round up a gang of saboteurs."

"Saboteurs!" exclaimed Harry. "Are there any in Mountchester?"

"There's been sabotage at the National Electric Co.," said the red-haired boy.

"How do you know?" inquired Tom. "And what's that about the G men."

"Do you remember Mr. Godfrey and Mr. Trainter?" asked Buddy as he and his chums neared the Martyne home.

"Sure!" exclaimed Tom and Harry added:

"They were after a gang the time we got locked in the big ice box and the girls rescued us."

"Well," continued Buddy, "Mr. Godfrey and Mr. Trainter are in Mountchester again. I saw them the other day. They were going in the electric plant. And G men don't hang around a small place like Mountchester unless there's something wrong going on."

"Saboteurs," murmured Tom.

"And the G men are after 'em," echoed Harry. "But what's our cipher got to do with that, Buddy?"

"I don't know—yet," the red-haired boy replied. "It's sort of a mystery but we helped the G men before and maybe we can again. And if we can, it may be useful for us to have a way of sending messages without anybody being able to read 'em, even if they find where we leave 'em."

"Where are we going to leave the cipher messages?" asked Tom.

"And you didn't finish telling us what Lysander of Sparta did with his cipher," said Harry.

"Lysander's cipher is the one I think we'll use," said Buddy. "It's simple but baffling to an outsider. It's what is called the stick and strip cipher. And here's where we're going to leave our ciphers."

As he spoke Buddy walked along a side path, half way between his house and the fish shack. The path was a short cut through a patch of woods. A short distance off the path Buddy stopped in front of a big oak tree. A short distance up the trunk was a hole where the bark and wood had rotted away, leaving a cavity.

"This will be a good cipher hideout," Buddy said. "It's near all our houses and the shack." He thrust his hand down into the cavity and brought up some dried, rotted wood and pieces of nut shells.

"Looks as if squirrels had a nest there," said Tom.

"Probably they have," said Buddy. "So much the better. Nobody will think of looking for our ciphers in a squirrel nest in an old, hollow tree. But come on and we'll start making a cipher as soon as my mother explains how to do it. She's got a book on all kinds of codes and ciphers."

Mrs. Martyne greeted Buddy and his chums. They lost no time in getting down to business.

"We want something the girls can't read," said Buddy.

"I don't believe they will be able to read the stick and strip cipher unless you let them in on the secret," said Buddy's mother.

Bringing out the book she had been reading, Mrs. Martyne told about two simple ciphers, out of the scores that are in existence. "Codes were too cumbersome for the boys to use," she said.

"A code," she explained, "is a way of sending secret messages by means of short words. A number of words are selected. Each one stands for another word or for a phrase. But for this you need a code book in order to translate the message."

"A cipher is somewhat simpler but can be just as secret. Now I'll tell you about two ciphers and you can take your choice. One is the grille or cardan device. You prepare a card like this."

Mrs. Martyne showed the boys a piece of cardboard divided into 36 small squares. Of the squares 10 were punched or cut out leaving holes which were numbered, seemingly in no regular order.

"Each of you must have one of these cards or grilles," she went on. "Now suppose you wanted to send the message 'Go Back Home,' but wanted to disguise it so no one but the holder of the grille could read it. You might write this message on a piece of paper."

Mrs. Martyne showed a type written slip which read:

"The goat is not in my shack nor is his harness but he is gone that is sure."

"Doesn't seem to make much sense," spoke Tom.

"Now read it, taking the letters that show in each cut-out square of the grille," said Mrs. Martyne, "and in the order of their numbers from one to ten. Put down the letters as you pick them out."

The boys placed the grille over the seemingly incomprehensible message. The letters from 1 to 10 were:

"GOBACKHOME."

"When you separate them," said Mrs. Martyne, "you get the message: 'Go Back Home.' It's very simple but a bit cumbersome and you might lose the grille, in which case you would be at a loss."

"What's the stick and strip cipher?" asked Buddy.

His mother handed him a long strip of paper on which appeared a jumble of letters. Buddy and his chums looked at them, shook their heads and looked again.

"Can you read the message?" asked Mrs. Martyne with a smile.

"Can't make head or tail of it," said Tom.

"Well," began Buddy's mother. "It's the same message as before, but made with the stick and strip cipher. This is—"

"Hark, please!" interrupted Buddy. "I hear some one coming."

"It's the girls!" whispered Tom.

"They're on the front steps!" added Harry.

"They've followed us—the sneaks!" exclaimed Buddy.

CHAPTER V

THE G MAN

MRS. Martyne, who held in her hand a small, round stick, stepped to the window and looked out on the porch.

"You needn't take a stick to the girls, mother," said Buddy with a little laugh. "We can get rid of 'em easier than that."

"How?" asked Tom.

"As I was saying," went on the red-haired boy in a loud voice, "this water rat and this muskrat we have here—"

"You needn't go to all that unnecessary work," said Mrs. Martyne with a laugh. "It isn't the girls."

"Who is it?" asked Buddy.

"It's a man," said his mother. "A stranger to me. Lola is going to answer the bell."

The bell rang at that moment and Lola Wagg, the maid, could be heard walking through the hall. Mrs. Martyne and Buddy and his chums could hear her saying:

"No, sir, Mr. Martyne isn't in. But Mrs. Martyne is and so are Buddy and his chums."

"Oh, I'd like to see them," the man's voice went on. "In fact I came to see them but I thought I had better first ask for Mr. Martyne. Will you please tell Mrs. Martyne and also Buddy and his chums, that I am Mr. Godfrey."

"The G man!" exclaimed Buddy as he recognized the name.

"That's right—the G man," murmured Tom.

"I wonder what he wants with us," said Harry.

"I think the best way to find out would be to have him in here," said Mrs. Martyne. "Yes, Lola," she went on to the maid. "You may show in Mr. Godfrey."

"I hope I'm not disturbing a meeting of the Victory Club or anything like that," said Mr.

Godfrey nodding at Buddy, Tom and Harry.

"Not at all," said Buddy. "Mother, may I present Mr. Godfrey, one of the G men who helped get us out of the locked ice box," and the red-haired boy motioned to Mrs. Martyne.

"I am very glad to meet Buddy's mother," said the G man. "I have already had the pleasure of meeting Mr. Martyne. But I seem to have interrupted something," he went on as he noticed the strip of paper Buddy was holding and the stick in Mrs. Martyne's hand.

"It's a cipher," said Buddy, "but we can't read it."

"Ciphers aren't intended to be read easily," said Mr. Godfrey.

"Can you make anything of this?" asked Buddy.

He handed to Mr. Godfrey the long, narrow strip of paper on which appeared these letters separated into what appeared to be meaningless words:

GZOPT KLOYT EX BQLV SRAT XYZ LCOF PJKOS

IHLZY TLOCX PZ MOS KEZTK

The G man looked at the letters and strange words on the strip of paper. Then he smiled at Mrs. Martyne and said:

"If I had the stick that goes with this I think I could read it. Is that the stick?" he asked.

"Yes," said Buddy's mother. "It's just a piece of window curtain roller."

Mr. Godfrey took the round stick in his hand, looked at both ends and then held it so the boys could see a little slot cut in the end that the G man now held uppermost.

Next Mr. Godfrey took the strip of paper from Buddy. He put the end containing the word GZOPT in the slit and then began winding the strip around the stick in a spiral; close-winding it so that no wood was left bare between one spiral circle and the next. Holding the lower end of the strip against the bottom of the stick, Mr. Godfrey looked at the cipher a few seconds and announced:

"The message is: 'GO BACK HOME.' Here, you boys can read it yourselves."

He gave the stick with the spiral wrapped strip of paper about it to Buddy, first fastening the lower end with a pin so it would not unwind.

"Read the letters that now appear in a straight up and down line," suggested the G man.

"Why, sure enough, it says 'GO BACK HOME' as plain as anything!" exclaimed the red-haired boy in delight.

"Let's look!" begged Tom and Harry.

The message was as plain to them as it had been to Buddy, to the G man and to Mrs. Martyne.

"And yet," went on Mr. Godfrey as he unwound the strip again and straightened it out, "no one, unless he had a stick of the proper diameter, could make head or tail of this cipher."

"Then this is a cipher, is it?" asked Buddy.

"One of the simplest and best," said the G man. "It was invented, so history tells us, or at least adapted, by Lysander of Sparta. Have you told them that story?" he asked Mrs. Martyne.

"I was going to, when you came in," she replied. "Perhaps you would like to relate it, Mr. Godfrey."

"No, I'll leave that to you," said the G man. "Meanwhile I'd like to use your telephone, if I may."

"It's in the hall," said Buddy's mother. "I'll show you and then I'll tell the boys about Lysander's cipher."

She returned to the room where Buddy and his chums waited, having closed the door leading into the hall to give Mr. Godfrey privacy while telephoning.

"I won't go into the history back of it all," said Mrs. Martyne. "But it was very necessary, at one time, for Lysander to get a message he was expecting from his home land, in order to know what course to take. He knew his enemies were conspiring, but did not know just what form this was to take. He knew his friends would try to communicate with him while he was in Persia where he was then staying. But could a messenger get through? And if he did would not his secret message be taken from him and read?

"That was the problem Lysander had to solve, but he had prepared for it some time before by means of a cipher. One day he was seriously meditating on whether he should return to Sparta or remain where he was. If he remained he might miss connections with the Greek army that he thought was being sent to him.

"While Lysander was thus meditating and worrying," went on Mrs. Martyne, "a slave was brought before him. The slave said he was one of four sent to Lysander with messages from the government at home. The slave did not know what had happened to his three companions. They had probably been killed. He, himself, had been put in prison until it was clear to his captors that the only message he carried was one written on the tablets used in those days. The message on the tablets, which were confiscated, merely told Lysander to observe properly a coming religious festival.

"But, left alone with the slave, Lysander had him remove his belt. It was a long, narrow one of soft leather and on the inside was what seemed to be a mere jumble of letters and words, just jargon, such as the priests of those days used to write on belts to give travellers as good-luck charms.

"Dismissing the slave, but keeping his belt, Lysander took from his own belt the baton he always carried as his emblem of office. Into a slit in the upper end of this baton, or stick, Lysander slipped one end of the slave's belt. He then wound the leather belt spirally around the baton, just as you boys saw the strip of paper wound around the curtain roller. And instantly Lysander had the message. Only it was not as simple as the message I made for you boys."

"What was Lysander's cipher message?" asked Buddy.

"It was word that some of those he trusted had played false," said Mrs. Martyne. "Some of Lysander's friends had been murdered, and he was to be falsely tried for bribery when he came back to Greece. And, since messages asking him to return to stand trial had not been answered, he was to be judged guilty in his absence and condemned.

"Having received this secret cipher, which indicated that his own messages previously sent had never reached their destination, Lysander knew what to do. He got aboard a fast galley and hurried home through the Aegean sea. His life was saved and the empire was saved by his prompt action. This is the first recorded use of a cipher in such circumstances," concluded Mrs. Martyne.

"Say, that was a fine story!" commented Tom.

"And we can use the same sort of cipher, can't we?" asked Harry.

"Why not?" asked Buddy's mother. "All you need is a strip of paper and a stick. Each one of you will have to have a stick of the same diameter always, or the deciphering of the message will not be correct."

"The girls will never get on to this!" boasted Tom.

"We can send messages to each other," said Harry, "wind 'em on our sticks and read 'em."

"And we can leave the message in the old—" began Buddy.

"Somebody's coming!" warned Tom.

CHAPTER VI

SABOTAGE

AGAIN it was a false alarm, for the person approaching the Martyne living room, where Buddy and his chums had learned about the strip and stick cipher was merely Mr. Godfrey. He had finished his telephone talk.

But from the worried and somewhat puzzled look on the face of the G man, Buddy and his chums surmised that all was not going well. However they knew they had no right to make inquiries.

Mr. Godfrey smiled at Mrs. Martyne, Buddy and his chums and asked:

"Well, do you boys think you can send cipher messages now?"

"Well, I guess we can by the stick and strip method and with the card grille," Buddy said.

"Oh, then you know about the grille?" asked the G man.

"I told them a little about it," said Mrs. Martyne. "But I thought they could have more fun with this other," and she indicated the stick and strip. "They only want to send unimportant personal communications among themselves," she added.

"Do G men use ciphers?" asked Buddy, thinking this a harmless question.

"Oh, yes," admitted Mr. Godfrey. "Mr. Trainter and I often communicate by cipher. And sometimes we let our ciphers fall into the hands of those we are trailing. But you may be sure they never get any real information from such messages."

"Is Mr. Trainter here in town with you?" asked Tom.

"Yes, he is," admitted Mr. Godfrey. "I didn't mean to let that out just yet. But I know I am among friends and loyal supporters of our government," he said more seriously. "Please don't talk about this, or about what I am going to speak to you about in a moment."

"We'll keep quiet about it," promised Harry and the other boys nodded in agreement.

"Is there a G case in town?" asked Buddy.

"That I can't answer," said Mr. Godfrey with a smile. "But you may do some guessing after I ask you a few questions."

"We heard," went on Tom, "there was some sabotage going on down at the National Electric Co."

"There is no secret about that," admitted the G man. "It has been in the papers. And I don't mind admitting that I would like to get on the trail of the saboteurs."

"Could we help?" asked Buddy eagerly.

"Well, you might," said Mr. Godfrey. "You aided Mr. Trainter and me before. You may again. But what I called for now is to ask if you boys know anything about an old shack down on the river. It seems to have been used as a sort of meeting place for a fishing club. It smells fishy and I don't mind telling you that something 'fishy,' in the sense of suspicious actions, have been going on in that neighborhood."

"Why, that's our shack!" exclaimed Buddy. "We boys used it for a meeting place until we took over part of our garage for the Victory Club."

"I hope you G men don't suspect us," said Tom.

"Oh, no!" laughed Mr. Godfrey. "I know you boys too well to think of that. But I believe the shack has been used without your knowledge as a place where secret and, I may say, cipher messages have been left by one person to be picked up later by another. This is a common method that criminals or saboteurs use to communicate with one another. It gets rid of the danger of a personal meeting."

"We don't know anything about this," said Buddy.

"I supposed you didn't," spoke the G man. "But I came to ask you to keep your eyes open in and around the shack."

"We haven't used it much, lately," said Tom.

"We were thinking of leaving our cipher messages there," said Harry, "so the girls couldn't read 'em. They know Morse code so they read our flashlight signals."

"I would think, because of blackouts, that flashlight signals couldn't be used," said Mr. Godfrey.

"They can't!" chuckled Buddy. "We found that out." He told of the air raid warden's warning.

"You can easily substitute the stick and strip cipher," said Mr. Godfrey. "Well, that's the reason I came here," he went on. "To ask you boys to keep your eyes open around the old fishing shack. Has it always been used for that?"

"I believe it has," said Mrs. Martyne.

"Some years ago there was a company that caught fish in the river to sell to dealers. The shack was their river office. The company failed, a receiver was appointed and Mr. Martyne's law office handled the matter. My husband is really the custodian and, you might say, owner of the shack and he let the boys use it."

"It is good to have this information," said Mr. Godfrey, making some notes in his book. "I'll leave the rest to you boys—at least for a time. If you see or hear anything suspicious, you might let me know. I am boarding at this address," and he wrote one down for Buddy and his chums. "Incidentially I am supposed to be employed at the electric plant. So is Mr. Trainter. We are on the watch there. You boys, between times of preparing your cipher messages for fun, may do some serious work by watching the shack."

"We will!" promised Buddy.

"I am disclosing no secret," went on the G

man, "when I say that many important electrical instruments made here in the Mountchester factory, have been secretly and mysteriously damaged by some one with access to them in the factory. So far we haven't been able to discover by whom. But these instruments are used on our planes and any tampering with them may cause serious and terrible accidents, either here, or when the planes are sent abroad to the fighting fronts."

"Saboteurs?" questioned Tom.

"Yes, saboteurs," snapped Mr. Godfrey. "It's dirty, underhand and sneaking work on the part of our enemies abroad who have agents here. We've got to discover them."

"And we'll help!" exclaimed the red-haired boy.

"We sure will!" echoed his chums.

"I think that is all now," said Mr. Godfrey. "Don't show too much open enthusiasm or activity," he warned. "By so doing you may tip off the saboteurs that we are on their trail.

Just be casual about it. I think your plan to use a simple cipher for sending each other messages that others can't read, may come in useful. Practice up on it. Maybe I can use it on this case."

"Gosh! That would be great!" exclaimed Buddy. And in his eagerness he leaped up and clicked his heels together three times.

"Pretty good!" laughed the G man. "Well, I'll see you later," he remarked as he prepared to leave.

"There's something I want to tell you," spoke Buddy. "There's a big oak tree, with a hollow in, between here and the shack. It's on a side path. We boys planned to leave cipher messages in it. Maybe we could leave some there for you. Would you like to see where it is?"

"I think it would be a good idea," agreed Mr. Godfrey. "Suppose you come now and point it out to me. That hollow tree may come in very useful."

"And when we come back," Buddy said to his mother, "we'll put in some practice on that stick and strip cipher."

"I'll have some material ready for you," Mrs. Martyne promised. "I think there are some more old curtain roller sticks out in the garage."

"But don't tell the girls!" begged Buddy.

"No, I won't," his mother promised. "Probably the girls will get up a cipher of their own when they learn you boys have one."

"Let 'em," said Tom.

"I'll bet we can read any cipher they make," boasted Harry.

"I wouldn't be too sure of that," cautioned Mr. Godfrey. "Some simple ciphers are hard to read. But of course an expert would be able to decipher them. Well, boys, let's get along to the hollow tree and see what sort of a hiding place it will make for secret messages."

The four were soon on the seldom-used path that led through the little patch of woods.

"Couldn't be better!" was the G man's verdict. "In a few days I may leave a message here for you. We'll decide on one of the stick and strip type. I'll give you the diameter of the stick to use. That, really, is the basis of the secret."

He reached over to put his hand down in the hollow of the old tree. A moment later he uttered an exclamation of pain and withdrew his hand quickly. From several fingers blood was dripping.

CHAPTER VII

A STRAY DOG

Buddy gasped in surprise as he saw Mr. Godfrey's bleeding hand.

"What happened?" asked the red-haired boy. "Is there a trap in the hollow? I didn't feel inside there myself. I just thought it was a good hiding place."

"It is—for a squirrel," said Mr. Godfrey with a somewhat rueful laugh.

"A squirrel!" Tom exclaimed.

"Yes," replied the G man. "I put my hand right into his nest and, naturally, he nipped me. There he goes, now."

Mr. Godfrey pointed to an angry, scurrying bushytail that was now on a tree branch over the heads of Buddy and the G man. And there the squirrel sat, scolding and chattering.

"I didn't know a squirrel had a nest in this tree," said Harry. "If they have, I guess we boys can't use it as a place to leave our cipher messages."

"Oh, yes you can," said the G man, shaking a few drops of blood from his fingers. "It will be all the better. If any of the saboteurs, or anyone else sees a squirrel going into this hollow, they will never guess it is being used as a hiding place for messages. But I think the squirrels won't be here long."

"Do you mean they'll leave because of the messages we boys might put in their nest?" Buddy asked.

"No, but this is now Summer," said Mr. Godfrey. "In the Summer squirrels generally make their home in nests near the tops of trees. The nests are almost as big as crows' nests. The squirrels gather a lot of loose sticks and leaves and make a sort of Summer bungalow high up in a tree. When cold weather comes, they return to their Winter home in a hollow tree.

"Look up, and you can see one of the Summer nests. I think this squirrel was just about moving out when we came here. He probably was sent back by his wife to make sure nothing was left behind when the move was made to the Summer nest."

"And you put your hand right on him," said Buddy.

"Almost in his mouth, I guess," chuckled the G man. "At any rate he nipped me and then scurried out to scold us."

"He sure is chattering away," commented Tom, as he looked up at the big nest of leaves and sticks, high in the tree. A little later the squirrel, evidently thinking he had sufficiently berated the intruders, scurried on up the tree and disappeared into the nest.

"Is it a bad bite?" asked Harry as Mr. Godfrey shook more drops of blood from his fingers.

"Oh, not so bad," was the reply. "But I suppose I had better put a little iodine on it. Only I haven't any with me."

"I know where there's some," Buddy said.

"Down in the fishing shack on the river. I saw a bottle there the other day when we boys were sort of cleaning out the place to use this Summer. I guess the men who used to work for the fish company used the iodine when they got a hook in their hands or when a fish bit them."

"Probably," agreed Mr. Godfrey.

"Maybe the bottle has been there some time," said Harry. "Do you think it is still good?"

"Oh, yes, I think so. Being a disinfectant it ought to keep a long time, if it's corked," said the G man.

"It's corked all right," Buddy said. "Come on to the shack and I'll give you a First Aid treatment."

"All right," assented Mr. Godfrey with a laugh.

Half way to the shack Buddy suddenly stopped and said:

"I've just thought of something, Mr. Godfrey."

"What's that, Buddy?"

"Suppose we boys leave cipher messages on paper, like the stick and strip system, won't the squirrels chew up the paper and spoil the cipher?"

"They might," admitted Mr. Godfrey. "But you can enclose the strip of paper in a small tin can. Sharp as squirrels' teeth are, they can't gnaw through tin."

"That's what we'll do—use a tin box," decided Buddy. "I'll tell the fellows. But now for the iodine."

Leaving the seldom-used path in the woods, Buddy, his chums and the G man were soon within sight of the shack on the river.

"I hope that iodine is still there," said Buddy. He was about to run on ahead to open the shack door, when Mr. Godfrey clapped his unbitten hand on the shoulder of the red-haired boy.

"Not so fast, Buddy," said the G man in a low voice.

"Why, what's the matter?"

"Never approach a place like this, when you are on the trail of saboteurs or other enemies, without reconnoitering a bit," advised the G man. "You never know what changes might have taken place since you were last there. I'll just fire a warning shot."

"You mean you're going to shoot?" asked Tom. He thought Mr. Godfrey would draw his gun, which Buddy knew he carried, and at least fire into the air. But, instead, the G man picked up a stone.

"I don't know how good an aim I can take with my left hand," he said to Buddy. "But I used to pitch on a ball team and I was as good a 'South-paw' as I was a 'North-paw,' which isn't saying such a lot. However, I'll have a go at it with my left hand. Stoop down back of the bushes, boys," he added, indicating a clump near where the two had come to a stop within sight of the shack and about 200 feet away.

"Why?" asked Buddy, who was a great one

for asking questions. "Do you think some one is in the shack and may open the door and fire at us?"

"You never can tell," said the G man. "Hide, boys."

The red-haired boy and his chums concealed themselves back of the bushes, but could look through the branches at the shack. They saw Mr. Godfrey pause a moment while keenly watching the old fish building.

Then, amid a silence broken only by the rustling of the woodland leaves and the distant murmur of the river, Mr. Godfrey threw the stone.

It struck the door of the shack squarely with a resounding thud.

"Not bad with my left hand, and I haven't used it much lately," said Mr. Godfrey with a chuckle. "Now to see what happens."

Buddy, Tom and Harry almost stood up behind their concealing bush as the echoes of the thumping stone died away.

The door of the shack did not open. Nor was there any burst of fire from either of the windows, one on each side of the door.

But from the interior of the shack came a series of loud barks.

"A dog!" exclaimed Buddy. "I wonder who left a dog in there?"

"Quiet, please," said Mr. Godfrey in a low voice. "Where there's a dog there are generally men—the two go together. And, though most dogs are good, I can't say the same for men. Let's wait a little longer before going any closer."

They waited. The dog continued to bark and from the volume of sounds he made Buddy concluded it was rather a large dog.

"Well, I guess it's safe," said Mr. Godfrey. "If there were men or even a man in the shack, he would either have given some sign by this time or he would have quieted the dog. Since the dog keeps on barking, it's my guess the animal is alone in the shack."

"Do you think some of the saboteurs may have left the dog on guard?" asked Tom.

"I hardly think so. There isn't anything in the shack to guard, as far as I know. And the spies or suspects, if they have used it, probably haven't been there lately, knowing you boys have been around the place. I think it's just a stray dog in the shack."

"But why would he stay there, all alone?" asked Harry.

"He was probably shut in and left there, or he may have wandered in by himself and can't get out. You notice the door is shut."

"Yes," said Buddy, "but it isn't locked. It doesn't lock from the inside and there's no pad-lock."

"Good observation," commended Mr. Godfrey. "I think it's safe to approach now. But we'll have to beware of the dog—at first."

As Buddy had observed, the shack door, though tightly closed, was not locked. Mr. Godfrey pushed it open cautiously. It opened inward.

No sooner was the door opened a small crack that a dog's nose was thrust out but, instead of challenging barks, came pitiful whinings and whimperings.

"The poor dog has been shut up here probably all night," said Mr. Godfrey. "He isn't a savage dog. If he was he'd be banging against the door, growling and barking. Instead he seems glad to see us."

"He's almost wagging his tail off," said Buddy with a laugh. Through the partly-opened door he could see in the shack a brown dog, evidently of the setter breed. And the lonely animal was now whimpering with joy and jumping about with fast-wagging tail.

"That tail is a good sign," said Mr. Godfrey, opening the door wider.

A moment later the dog, a Gordon setter, leaped out with a joyous bark. First he sniffed at Mr. Godfrey's legs, then at Buddy's.

And, as if satisfied with this reconnaissance, the dog, a moment later, was doing his best to use his tongue as a wash rag on Buddy's face.

"Down! Down!" commanded the red-haired boy with a laugh. But the stray dog was so happy at being let out by his new friends that he almost overwhelmed Buddy with his loving demonstrations.

"Gosh, he's a fine dog!" said Tom.

"I wish he was mine," said Harry.

"This dog," announced Buddy firmly, "is mine!"

CHAPTER VIII

TEST CIPHERS

AFTER having worked off some of his joy on Buddy, with a little side demonstration for Tom, Harry and the G man, the dog quieted down a bit. He sat outside the shack, his tongue hanging from his open, panting mouth.

Then, with a little bark, as if he had just thought of something, the dog ran to the river and lapped up the water eagerly.

"Poor fellow," commented Mr. Godfrey, "he probably hasn't had a drink in a long time."

"Nor anything to eat, either, I guess," said Buddy. "There are some cans of sausage in the shack. Tom, Harry and I were going to have a little picnic with them after we got this place in order. But I'm going to feed—I wonder what his name is?" he asked, indicating the setter. The dog had come back from the river, water dribbling from his mouth.

"He hasn't any collar on," commented Mr. Godfrey, "or we might be able to trace him. Either he's a stray or somebody stole him and may have hidden him in the shack. Looks like a good dog."

"I'll say he is!" exclaimed Buddy. And at the sound of the boy's admiring voice, the dog again leaped at Buddy and cavorted around him. "I wish you were really my dog," said the red-haired boy, wistfully.

"No reason why he can't be, for a while," said the G man. "At least until some one claims him. He seems to have taken a liking to you."

"And I like him," said Buddy. "I always liked dogs. I've had two or three, but not lately. Gosh, but I hope I can keep you, old fellow!" He pulled and fondled the dog's ears and the animal went into spasms of loving joy.

"Well, we'll leave the dog mystery to be

solved a little later," said Mr. Godfrey. "My own theory is that he has either been stolen and abandoned or has strayed away from home. He saw this shack. Maybe the door was open, or he may have pushed it open to get in. Once in he couldn't get out and he's been a prisoner ever since."

"First let's get the iodine for your hand," said Buddy, "then I'll open a can of sausages for—I wonder what I'll call my dog?" he spoke reflectively.

"Better wait a while until you see how long you can keep him," said Mr. Godfrey. "A name will be easily enough thought of. Now where is the iodine, Buddy?"

The red-haired boy produced the bottle from a wall cupboard. Mr. Godfrey decided the disinfectant was sufficiently fresh to use and put a generous amount on the squirrel bites.

"It stings," he said, wincing a bit. "I think it must be strong enough to combat any sort of germs. This will be quite a meeting place for you boys," he added as he let the surplus iodine drip from his fingers.

"Yes," Buddy agreed, "it will be all right if the saboteurs don't infest our shack. Maybe my dog will help keep 'em out."

"He might," assented the G man. "But I'm afraid he's too friendly to make a good watch dog. Setters aren't cut out for that work. Do you see any signs, Buddy, of strangers having been here since you and your chums were last in the shack?"

"No, I don't," Buddy answered. "It looks just the same. Except that the dog has knocked some things around."

"Probably trying to find a way out," said Mr. Godfrey.

The setter was now in the middle of the shack, looking from Mr. Godfrey to Buddy and thumping his tail on the floor.

"I guess that means you're hungry," Buddy said. "I'll get you some sausage."

From another wall cupboard the red-haired boy took a can and, opening it, turned out some savory sausages on a tin plate he got from what served as the little kitchen.

The dog made short work of the canned meat. Then he wagged his tail in appreciation and trotted down to the river for another drink.

"I wonder if he'll bring back a stick," said Buddy. "I'll try him." He tossed a stick into the river, pointed to it and said: "Bring it here!"

The dog leaped in and was soon vigorously swimming toward the floating piece of wood.

"He sure can go some," chuckled Mr. Godfrey as the dog came back, dropping the stick at Buddy's feet. Then, like the well-bred animal he evidently was, he went off a little distance and shook himself to rid his long coat of surplus water.

"Yes, he certainly can go some," said Mr. Godfrey again.

Suddenly Buddy jumped into the air and clicked his heels together three times.

"What's that for?" asked Mr. Godfrey with

a laugh. He knew Buddy well enough, now, to be sure the heel-clicking indicated something.

"You just gave me a name for my dog," Buddy said.

"I did?" asked the G man.

"Yes. You said he can 'go some.' Well, I'm going to use that name. But I'll spell it all in one word 'GOSUM.' How's that for a name?"

"Couldn't be better. Could it, Gosum?" he asked, snapping his iodine-stained fingers at the setter.

In a moment the dog was leaping about Mr. Godfrey, trying to lick the brown hand.

"None of that!" laughed the G man. "I need that iodine to counteract the squirrel bite. But you sure are a good dog, Gosum."

"He knows his name already," laughed Buddy. "Here, Gosum," he called. "Fetch it!"

Another stick, thrown into the river, was quickly brought back. And then, after another shake, to rid himself of water, Gosum seemed to quiet down and watched for Buddy's next command. He paid small attention to Tom or Harry.

After an inspection in and about the shack, Mr. Godfrey said there was nothing suspicious connected with it as yet. He and the boys both agreed to the theory that Gosum was just a stray, but a good dog, who had wandered into the shack.

"And I'm going to take him home," said Buddy.

"Might as well," agreed the G man. "You may see an advertisement from his owner or you may hear about a lost dog. Until then—keep Gosum."

The dog wagged his tail in apparent recognition of his new name.

Mr. Godfrey left Buddy and his chums, saying he was going to the factory of the National Electric Co. He and Mr. Trainter, his F.B.I. partner were working there, under cover, trying to trace the spies and saboteurs who were seeking to undermine our country's war effort.

"I'll see you again, soon, boys," said Mr. Godfrey as he parted from the red-haired boy and his chums. "Meanwhile you and your friends can practice on the strip and stick code. Keep to that. It's simple but it's good. Meanwhile I'll work out that size stick to use so we can exchange secret messages."

"My mother said an ordinary stick from a roller curtain would make a good stick," said Buddy.

"So it would. They are easily obtainable. But we must be sure the diameters are all the same, else the message wound about the stick will be all garbled. You let me know the diameter of the curtain sticks you and your chums will use and Mr. Trainter and I will get some the same size."

"I'll do that," Buddy promised. "Come on, Gosum," he called. The setter, with a farewell wag of his tail at the G man, followed his red-haired master.

"He sure is a good dog," commented Harry.

"Never saw a better. Hi, Gosum!" said Tom.

The dog fawned upon Buddy's chums and on the red-haired boy, and there was a happy trio with the lone setter.

Gosum soon made himself at home in Buddy's house and in the garage club of the members of the Victory Club. Mrs. Martyne readily consented to allow Buddy to keep the dog.

"At least until his owner claims him," she added.

"I hope he never does," Buddy said.

Several days passed. No one claimed Gosum and there was no advertisement in the local or nearby papers about a lost setter.

"I guess I can keep you, Gosum," said Buddy. "And, Oh, boy! Am I glad!"

Evidently, from his manner, the dog was, also.

In the next week Buddy and his chums worked diligently at perfecting themselves in their cipher work. They adopted a standard-sized curtain stick, a piece about 15 inches long, about which to roll the long tape or strip of paper that, at first sight, seemed to contain only a meaningless jumble of letters.

Buddy gave Mr. Godfrey and Mr. Trainter the stick dimensions and several test ciphers were exchanged between the two G men and Buddy and his chums. The messages were concealed in the hollow tree, placed in a tin can for safety from the squirrels. Though, as a matter of fact, the bushytails seemed to have taken up their Summer residence in the high nest.

The test messages were of no particular moment, but served to perfect the boys in their cipher work. Each one had a stick and at one end was a mark. On this mark was placed the end of the long strip of paper, which also had a mark to indicate the starting place. But anyone finding the strip would not be able to read it unless he or she possessed the right sized stick. That was the trick.

Meanwhile Gosum was seemingly reconciled to his new home and new master.

One day Mr. Godfrey left in the hollow tree a message which, when wrapped about the stick, was translated to read:

"BE ON THE ALERT."

"Something's in the wind, boys," said Buddy who took out the cipher and communicated it to his chums. "Something's going to happen."

"Something has happened!" exclaimed Tom who, with Harry, had come over to Buddy's house.

"What?" asked the red-haired boy.

"My sister and Harry's sister and I think your cousin Agnes, are on to our cipher," said Tom gloomily.

CHAPTER IX

"WHO GOT FOOLED?"

BUDDY and Harry were, for a moment, much surprised and disappointed at Tom's news.

"What makes you think my sister is onto our cipher?" asked Harry.

"Because," answered Tom, "your sister and my sister are over at our house now, making mysterious remarks and they looked at me in a funny way when I started out to come over here."

"Looking at you in a funny way doesn't mean anything," said Buddy.

"Oh, no?" jeered Tom. "You should have seen what they had and heard what they said."

"What?" asked Harry and Buddy together.

"Well, in the first place, they had some of the strips of our ciphers that we had left in the hollow tree."

"How did they get 'em?" asked Buddy.

"Do they know about the hollow tree?"

"I hope a squirrel bit 'em if they stuck their hands in the hole," growled Harry.

"I guess that part is my fault," Tom said.

"You didn't show 'em the tree, did you?" demanded Buddy, indignantly.

"No, but I guess I left in my room that last cipher message we wrote. I generally hide 'em under the rug but I forgot this time. And my sister got the strip of paper."

"Did they read it?" asked Harry.

"I don't know," said Tom, gloomily. "But my sister held up the strip and a piece of wood and said:

" 'We can read ciphers as well as you boys. We have this one all decoded. Ha! Ha! Who got left?' "

"What did my sister say?" asked Harry.

"She just laughed," commented Tom.

"Was my cousin Agnes there?" Buddy wanted to know.

"She sure was. She was winding the paper

strip around a piece of wood. My sister must have sneaked up and watched me through the key hole of the door."

"That's tough luck," said Harry.

Buddy gave a tug at his red hair and asked:

"Did they say what the message was?"

"No," admitted Tom. "They didn't. I said they couldn't read it and I dared them to read it to me. But they just laughed."

"Then they didn't read it?" asked Buddy.

"No," said Tom.

"What kind of a stick did they have?" asked Buddy.

"A square stick."

"Ha! Ha!" laughed the red-haired boy. "Then our secret is safe. They can't read our cipher unless they wind it around a stick that is circular, like a curtain stick. A square stick is no good. They were just bluffing."

"Golly, I think Buddy is right!" exclaimed Harry.

"I hope so," said Tom. "I was thinking it was all my fault."

"Well, we've got to be more careful," said Buddy. "But everything is O.K. so far. Let the girls think they have discovered our cipher. But they haven't. It is still safe. And a good thing, too. For Mr. Godfrey will probably be sending us a secret message soon. One thing we've got to do, though."

"What?" asked Buddy's two chums.

"We've got to throw the girls off the track."

"How?" asked Tom and Harry.

"By doing as the G men do—let a fake message fall into their hands. We'll write out a cipher message and leave it where the girls will find it. But we'll sort of half-hide it so they think they have discovered it by accident. We'll give 'em a cipher message they can read all right."

"You mean a stick and strip cipher?" asked Tom.

"That'll give away all our plans," said Harry.

"No," chuckled Buddy, "we'll make up a grille cipher and let the girls have it with the de-coding card. They'll be so excited over thinking they have discovered our real cipher that they'll never try to work the stick and strip, even if they find it."

For a moment Tom and Harry thought over what Buddy had said. Then Tom asked:

"Think it'll work?"

"Sure," replied the red-haired boy. "It's regular G man tactics. Once let the other side think they have something, they'll be so tickled they won't bother about the real thing. Now let's get busy. We want to throw the girls off our trail before the real work of helping the G men catch the saboteurs starts."

"Do you really think we can be of help to the G men?" asked Tom.

"Mr. Godfrey wouldn't have sent us that cipher message about being on the alert unless there was something doing," Buddy declared.

"No, I suppose not," agreed Tom.

"I hope it will be as exciting as the time we got shut up in the old ice box," said Harry.

"It may be," was Buddy's opinion.

"The girls helped us then," spoke Tom in a sort of dreamy voice.

"So what?" asked Buddy.

"Maybe it's sort of mean to fool 'em on a cipher," Tom went on.

"We're just going to let them fool themselves," Buddy chuckled. "If they want to snoop into our affairs, trying to read our ciphers, we'll give 'em one they can read. But it won't amount to anything. Now let's get busy."

The boys, before deciding to use the strip and stick cipher, had experimented with the grille variety. They had made several masks of cardboard with the ten cells punched out. These cards, when placed over another card, containing what purported to be a message of no particular account, enabled one in the secret to read the hidden cipher.

For the next few days, between times of going on little trips with Gosum, the three boys worked on grille ciphers.

Besides making trips with the setter to the fish shack and the old, hollow tree, Buddy spent some time training his new dog. Gosum was clever. It needed only a few lessons to teach him to go to Buddy's home, from a considerable distance, when his master gave the order:

"Home, Gosum!"

Sometimes the setter was reluctant to leave Buddy. But the red-haired boy insisted and finally Gosum obeyed.

"You never can tell," Buddy said to his chums, "when I might be in trouble and want to send Gosum for help. If I don't make him mind me now, he won't mind me then."

"Suppose you were in trouble," proposed Tom, "and sent Gosum home for help. How would your folks know that your dog was asking that help be sent you?"

"Laugh that one off, Buddy," chuckled Harry.

"It's easy," said Buddy. "I'd just tie a message on Gosum's collar, tell him to go home, say if I was caught in a trap or held captive. My father or mother would read the message and come and help me."

"But Gosum hasn't a collar," Tom pointed out.

"I'm going to get one for him," said Buddy. "And now let's work out a cipher with a grille that will be read by the girls but which will fool them."

Carrying out this plan, Buddy and his chums, for several days, worked at ciphers in the open, right under the noses of the three girls, so to speak.

"You think you can fool us with your secret ciphers," teased Agnes Randall.

"Oh, maybe we can," said her cousin Buddy.

It happened three days after this. Agnes hurried to tell Lucy and Mary the big news.

"Look!" exclaimed Agnes, holding out some papers.

"What is it?" asked Lucy.

"It's a secret cipher the boys think we can't read," said Agnes.

"I don't believe we can," spoke Mary. "I found some papers scattered around Harry's room. I tried to read what was on them but it didn't make sense."

"A cipher never does unless you know how to decode it," said Agnes. "But I was over at Buddy's house. I was walking through the hall and I picked up these papers. At first I didn't know what they were but when I looked at them I found they made a cipher message."

"What does it say?" asked Lucy.

"I haven't translated it yet," went on Agnes. "But this is the message." She held out a paper on which were the words, arranged in several lines:

"When he tries to fall out
going home some one
listening may be driving."

"Utter trash, if you ask me," said Lucy.

"Doesn't make sense," added Mary.

"Not until you use this," said Agnes, producing a card in which several holes were cut. "This is a grille," she explained. "I know because I found a book in Aunt Martyne's room and it told about grille ciphers. Now all we have to do is to put this card, with the holes cut in it, over this message which doesn't mean anything, and we can get at the real meaning. Like this:"

Agnes put the grille over the strange message. Through the holes in the upper card the girls read this:

"WHO GOT FOOLED?"

CHAPTER X

HI-JACKED

FOR a few moments Lucy Gordon and Mary Clee divided their looks of surprise between the grille cipher and Buddy's cousin. Then Mary said:

"Well, I don't see what this means?"

"Don't you?" asked Lucy.

"And I don't, either," chimed in Agnes.

"It means just what it says," went on Lucy. "The boys fooled us, and this is their way of letting us know it."

"Fooled us—how?" spluttered Agnes, who seemed a bit angry.

"By letting us find this cipher and putting on it a message to let us know how silly we were," Lucy said. "This isn't their real, secret cipher. They must have another. I thought this was too easy to be the real thing."

"Well, of all the mean tricks!" exploded Agnes.

"We'll get even with the boys!" threatened Mary.

"It was partly our fault," said Lucy with a smile. "I suppose we had no business trying to find out their secret code."

"I think we had, after the way we helped them out the time they got locked in the big ice box. But I suppose they forget all about that and how we helped with the Victory Club," spoke Agnes.

"No, I don't believe they've forgotten that," said Lucy. "But it's natural they don't want us to know all their secrets, any more than we would want them to know ours. Besides, I think this cipher has something to do with the F.B.I."

"You mean G men?" asked Mary and Agnes, somewhat awed.

"Yes," continued Lucy. "I heard my brother telling Buddy something about F.B.I.

work. And I know that two G men—the same ones that were here after the boys got locked in the ice box—are in town again."

Agnes deliberately tore up the grille cipher which had carried such a mocking message.

"What's the idea?" asked Lucy.

"I'm not going to be mixed up with G men," said Agnes. "It's too dangerous."

"Oh, I don't imagine this silly little cipher has anything to do with Buddy's G man mystery and the real cipher," said Lucy. "The G men have some other way of sending secret messages."

"I know," said Agnes. "It has something to do with a stick and a strip of paper. Maybe we can—"

"Let's drop it," advised Lucy. "I tried to make some sense of a stick and strip I found in Tom's room. But—no soap."

"Well, then, let's drop it," agreed Mary. "Anyhow, if we're going to Sally Marton's lawn party we'd better be thinking up some new games to play."

"And forget about the cipher," agreed Lucy.

"All right," assented Agnes. "But I don't like Buddy to be crowing over me."

However Buddy and his chums didn't taunt the girls with falling into the cipher trap. As a matter of fact, though they knew their trick had worked, neither Buddy, Tom nor Harry referred to the affair. They found the torn scraps of the grille and "Who got Fooled?" message but did not speak of it.

One reason was that the same day, in the hollow tree, Buddy found a strip and stick cipher from Mr. Godfrey. That is he found the rolled up strip of paper, with strange words on it, in the tin box in the hollow tree. Losing no time, Buddy hurried home and got out the piece of curtain stick.

Winding the paper around it, with the little mark at the top coinciding with the mark on the top of the stick, Buddy twisted the paper around until it completely covered the stick, spiral fashion.

Slowly the red-haired boy read off the letters that appeared in a vertical line. He set them down on paper and divided them into words. Then, uttering a slight exclamation of surprise, Buddy ran down stairs to the telephone. He first called Tom.

"It's come," was Buddy's first remark.

"What?" Tom asked.

"A cipher from Mr. Godfrey. The saboteurs are going to pull off something tonight."

"What?"

"They're going to try to hijack a shipment of valuable electric parts from the factory."

"Whew!" whistled Tom, shrilly over the telephone.

"Come over to my house," said Buddy, "and bring Harry."

The three boys were soon looking at the cipher still on the stick where Buddy had wound it. Read down, vertically, was the message:

"Be at shack. Hijacking tonight."

It was signed with a small triangle containing a single dot. This was Mr. Godfrey's way of letting Buddy and his chums know the message was authentic. Mr. Trainter's signature was a small square containing a small circle.

"I wonder what we'd better do?" asked Harry.

"Be at the shack, of course," said Buddy promptly.

"But if there's going to be a gang of hijackers there," went on Harry, "it may be dangerous. Not that I'm afraid of danger, but the G men promised our folks, when they asked permission for us to help on this case, that we wouldn't be put in danger."

"I don't believe we will be," said Buddy. "Naturally there may be a little danger. Hijackers aren't exactly good men to mix up with. But I think Mr. Godfrey only wants us to help in a way that wouldn't put us in too much danger."

"How can we find out what he really wants us to do?" asked Tom.

"I'm going to telephone him," Buddy said. "I have his number, at the place where he boards. You know he and Mr. Trainter are working, under assumed names, at the electric plant. I'll get him on the wire at supper time and he'll tell us what to do."

"Gosh, this is getting exciting!" murmured Harry.

"Hijackers! I should say so!" commented Tom.

Buddy's reaction was to jump up and click his heels together three times.

As the occasion seemed to warrant it, Buddy had his two chums stay for supper at his house that night. At the hour he had agreed on previously with Mr. Godfrey, Buddy called the G man at his boarding house. There was a little delay until Mr. Godfrey came to the telephone. Then, Buddy, in as casual voice as he could manage, said:

"Did you want to go fishing tonight?"

"Might not be a bad idea," said Mr. Godfrey. "We're after some night-walkers."

"Yes, those worms make good bait," Buddy

said. "We'll meet you there—all three of us."

"And don't worry if we don't get any bites," went on the G man. "The moon may not be just right for fishing," he added with a chuckle. "But you may see a little fun. And, by the way, do you mind if I send a friend to meet you at the fishing pier?"

"Not at all," said Buddy. By this he knew that another G man than Mr. Trainter was to be in on that night's work.

"At 8 o'clock then," said Mr. Godfrey. "Watch for a man with a feather in his hat."

"Well?" Buddy's chums asked him, suppressed excitement in their voices, as Buddy left the telephone.

"It's all set," said the red-haired boy. "We are to go to the shack to help catch the hi-jackers. Look out for a man with a feather in his hat."

CHAPTER XI

THE MOTOR BOAT

TOM, who had picked up the secret cipher warning about the hijacking, to read it again, laid it aside to ask:

"What's this about a man with a feather in his hat?"

"I think it must be another G man," said Buddy. "Mr. Trainter and Mr. Godfrey are probably covering one end of the hijacking operations, and they had to get another man for the river shack end. There was no time to introduce us to this third G man so he is to wear a feather in his hat so we'll know him."

"That's a good idea," commented Tom.

"I notice," said Harry, "that you didn't speak about anything like hijacking over the wire."

"Of course not," said Buddy. "You can't

tell who would be listening. There may be spies even in the place where Mr. Godfrey boards. He told me, when I telephoned, to talk casual like, about something natural. So I pretended we were just going fishing."

"That was clever," said Tom.

"Oh, I'm full of clever ideas," chuckled the red-haired boy. "And now we'll get ready to go to the shack."

"This strange code and cipher business is already beginning to pay dividends," said Harry.

"Oh, we haven't done anything yet," Buddy remarked. "Wait until after tonight."

The parents of Buddy and his two chums were a little hesitant about allowing the three boys to go to the river shack that night, when some hijacking operations might be in preparation.

"I think it's too risky," Mrs. Martyne said, when Buddy had told her of his talk with Mr. Godfrey.

The same objection was made at the homes of Tom and Harry.

"But there won't be any danger," Buddy pleaded. "The G men will take all the risks."

"I'm not so sure of that," said Mrs. Martyne. "Of course I want you to be patriotic, Buddy, and help our war effort all you can. But this seems a little too dangerous."

"Really it isn't, Mother," Buddy said earnestly. "Mr. Godfrey wouldn't let us get into danger. Don't you remember the other time, when he and Mr. Trainter caught the gang, after we had been locked in the ice box, we boys had to stay back beyond the danger line."

"But this time you tell me he wants you actually to help catch hijackers," said Mrs. Martyne.

"I don't believe we boys will be lucky enough actually to catch any hijackers," Buddy said. "I don't know just what Mr. Godfrey wants us to do. But if I get him on the wire again, and he tells you it's all safe, will you let me go."

"Yes, if he assures me you will not be in danger," said Mrs. Martyne, "I'll let you go."

"You can talk to Mr. Godfrey yourself," said Buddy.

Once more the G man was on the wire. He spoke to Mrs. Martyne saying:

"We only want the boys as watchers at a certain place. We have to divide our forces tonight, and we may need the boys to act as messengers, that's all. I'll make sure they are in no real danger."

With that promise Mrs. Martyne was content and so were the other parents. Shortly before 8 o'clock, Buddy and his chums started for the old shack on the river bank. It was a cloudy evening which made it darker than would otherwise have been the case. There was a full moon but the clouds seemed to be doing their best to hide it.

"Is Gosum coming?" asked Tom as he and Harry met at Buddy's house and the setter appeared, wagging his tail.

"Sure he's coming," Buddy answered.

"He may bark at the wrong time," objected Harry.

"He won't bark if I tell him to keep quiet," said the red-haired owner of Gosum. Buddy had great faith in his dog.

"I see you got a collar for him," remarked Harry as the three boys and the dog neared the shack.

"It's really two collars," said Buddy.

"What do you mean?" asked Tom.

"Look," said Buddy. "It's a sort of double collar with a secret compartment."

He called Gosum back to him, for the dog had wandered on a little way in advance. Then Buddy showed his chums how a flap of leather, running half way around the collar, could be pulled to one side. There was room between the flap and the real collar to put a strip of paper.

"Here's the idea," said Buddy. "You remember how the slave from Sparta carried the cipher message to Lysander in his belt. Well, maybe Gosum will take a cipher message from me in his double collar. It's just a chance,'' Buddy concluded as he fastened the flap on the dog's collar back in place. A casual glance would not disclose that it was there.

''Very clever,'' complimented Tom.

''Yes, Buddy is full of cleverness,'' chuckled Harry.

''Well, I only hope the G man are clever enough to catch the hijackers,'' remarked the red-haired lad.

''What are you turning off here for?'' asked Tom as Buddy, who was in the lead, veered to a side path through the woods.

''I thought we'd stop at the hollow tree and see if there was a last-minute cipher message,'' Buddy answered. ''I brought the stick with me,'' he added, showing it.

''I hope there's no message calling this off,'' said Tom.

''Same here,'' remarked Harry. ''I'm all set for hijackers.''

"Maybe we won't even see 'em," Buddy said. "Mr. Godfrey says even the best plans the G men make sometimes fail."

"Let's hope this one won't," said Tom. "I'd like to see these German rats of saboteurs caught."

"So would I," echoed Buddy and Harry.

There was no message, cipher or other, in the hollow tree so the boys went on to the shack. It seemed silent and deserted, perched on the bank close to the river, with a small float in front, for the river often rose during Spring floods.

"Doesn't seem to be anybody there," said Tom.

"Not even the new G man with a feather in his hat," spoke Harry.

"You can't tell," remarked Buddy in a low voice. "I'll try the stone signal before we go any closer to the shack."

Buddy tossed a stone which thudded against

the locked door. The boys had put a padlock on the shack and each one carried a key. The three waited and listened. Buddy threw another stone. There was still no sign of life.

"I guess it's all right," said Tom.

"No," spoke Buddy in a low voice. "We'll give it another test. Nothing like being sure."

"What are you going to do next?" asked Harry.

"Here, Gosum," spoke Buddy to his dog in a low voice. "Go smell 'em out! See if anybody's there. Go to the shack."

Gosum looked up at his master in the light of the moon which, for a moment, shone through a rift in the clouds. Then, wagging his tail, as if to say he understood, the setter cautiously went down to the shack. He sniffed at the door, walked all round it, still sniffing, and then without barking a warning, came back to Buddy. The tail was wagging harder than before.

"Now I'm pretty sure it's all right," said Buddy. "We can go to the shack and wait for something to happen."

"Gosum sure is a smart dog," said Tom, as he gently pulled the setter's ears.

"Well, who trained him?" demanded Buddy, with just a little justifiable pride in his voice.

The shack was still silent and dark as the boys approached it. But there was no alarming scramble of feet, which might indicate uninvited visitors, as Buddy put his key in the lock and swung open the door.

"Nobody home," remarked Tom.

"Except us," added Buddy.

"Is there anything to eat here?" asked Harry.

"Some crackers and cheese, I think," said Buddy. "I left some here last time. And there's some bottles of ginger ale, but they won't be very cold."

"We can tie strings to the necks of the bottles and let them dangle in the river a little while," suggested Tom. "That'll cool 'em off a bit."

"Good idea," complimented Buddy. "Wait until I make a light."

There were several lamps and a lantern in the shack. As there was no reason as yet, for concealing their presence in their rendezvous, the boys soon had the lights going. Buddy found the crackers and cheese, which were kept in a tin box as protection against river rats, and Tom and Harry soon had several bottles of ginger ale cooling in the river at one end of the float.

"And now to wait for what happens," said Buddy as he sat down, Gosum curled at his feet. The dog had made a tour inside the shack and seemed satisfied, after many suspicious sniffings, that all was well.

"I wonder what's really going on?" asked Tom as the three were munching crackers and cheese a little later, and sipping the ginger ale, which wasn't too warm.

"If it's anything like what Mr. Godfrey

first told us," said Buddy, "this may be another attempt to get some of the valuable electric instruments that the factory is shipping to our forces abroad."

"What sort of instruments are they, I wonder?" asked Harry.

"Oh, maybe a new kind of bomb sight, or some jigger for detecting submarines—I wouldn't know," said Buddy.

"I hope the G men catch the rats," said Tom.

As if the word "rats," recalled something to him, Gosum suddenly growled and started up.

"Quiet!" Buddy ordered his dog. Getting up softly, the red-haired boy opened the door of the shack and looked down to the float.

"It's a motor boat," said Buddy in a low voice to his chums.

CHAPTER XII

THE CHASE

SILENTLY tiptoeing to Buddy's side, as he stood in the doorway, Tom and Harry also looked down toward the river. They saw a good-sized motor craft silently sliding up to the float. Evidently the pilot, whoever he was, had cut the engine to let his craft drift the last few hundred feet. There had been no sound of the motor.

"Wonder who it is?" whispered Tom.

"Maybe the man with the feather in his hat," said Harry. "We'd better douse the glims until we're sure."

He turned back to put out the lamps, but Buddy checked him, saying:

"It's too late for that now. They've seen our lights." Then he hailed:

"Who are you; what do you want?"

From the motor boat a man's voice replied:

"I'm circle and cross from triangle and square. Who are you?"

"I'm V for Victory Club," Buddy answered.

"Then I'm at the right shack," went on the man's voice. "I made one mistake this evening. I guess the man who heard me reply, as I just answered you, Buddy, must have thought I was an escaped lunatic."

"So you know my name?" inquired the red-haired boy.

"Yes. And I suppose Tom Gordon and Harry Clee are with you?"

"Right," answered the owners of those two names. And Tom inquired in a whisper of Buddy:

"Who is he?"

Low as was Tom's voice, it carried, as sounds do better on, or near, water, and the pilot of the motor boat answered:

"I'm the man with the feather in his hat."

"Mind if I take a look?" asked Buddy.

"Go ahead," chuckled the man.

Buddy had a small but powerful flashlight with a searching beam. This he now focused on the man who was in the bow of the craft. He was holding it to the float with a boat hook. The beam of light shone on a long, white feather, jauntily adorning the hat of the man.

"It may not seem just the proper thing to be showing the white feather," said the man, "but I thought you might want to see it, and white is the most conspicuous color at night."

"Sure is," commented Buddy as he switched off his flashlight.

"I'm Mr. Bernard Weston," went on the wearer of the white feather as he disembarked to the float and quickly made his boat fast fore and aft.

"Yes, Mr. Godfrey told me to expect you," said Buddy.

"Then we're all set," went on Mr. Weston.

"I'll come up to the shack and tell you what's in the wind. It may blow or it may not—you never can tell."

As the new G man walked from the float up to the shack, Tom asked Buddy:

"What did all that mean—'circle and cross from triangle and square,' and you saying you were 'V for Victory Club?' What's the mysterious idea?"

"Mr. Godfrey's secret signature, as you saw, is a dot in a triangle," explained Buddy. "Mr. Trainter uses a little circle in a small square. Mr. Godfrey told me the new G man, who would have a feather in his hat, used the signature of a small circle with a cross in it. That's how I knew. And Mr. Godfrey said our secret sign of recognition with the G men would be to answer V for Victory Club if we had to answer a hail."

"Then it worked out all right," said Tom.

"It sure did," said Buddy.

"Do we have a secret signature to our ciphers?" asked Harry.

"Just a letter V upside down," said Buddy. "I have my own special signature. I'll tell you, or show you, later."

"I only hope our victory doesn't have an upside down," remarked Mr. Weston who had listened to this explanation.

"We'll do our best not to let that happen," said Buddy. "But is anything likely to happen tonight?"

"And can we help?" asked Tom.

"I can answer 'yes,' to both questions," said Mr. Weston. "It's a chance, though, at best. When we get to the shack I'll tell you all about it."

Inside the shack, after Gosum had been properly introduced to the G man and had approved of him, Buddy offered what hospitality there was—crackers and cheese and ginger ale.

"Just what I like!" said Mr. Weston heartily. "I haven't had any supper yet, but this will nicely fill the hole in my stomach. Quite a cozy little place you have here," he went on as he sat down and began to munch crackers and cheese while looking about the shack.

"We're going to fix it up better," said Buddy.

"We have a fine club house up in Buddy's garage," said Tom.

"Only the girls come there and they don't often get down here; that's why this place is better," commented Harry.

"Oh, girls aren't so bad," chuckled Mr. Weston. "And, from what I heard from Mr. Godfrey and Mr. Trainter, they did you a good turn the last time you helped us G men."

"Yes, they did," Buddy admitted. "But we don't want the girls mixing up with our cipher messages."

"You certainly have a right to some secrets," said Mr. Weston as he poured out a drink of ginger ale.

"Oh, we have the girls stopped there!" chuckled Tom.

Having finished his little meal, Mr. Weston was ready to talk to the boys.

"The idea is just this," he said. "We have discovered, from having observed several men under suspicion in the electric plant, that an attempt will be made tonight to hijack a valuable shipment of airplane and submarine parts. The shipment was sent from the factory a little while ago on a truck in charge of some trusted men. But the saboteurs plan to hold them up somewhere along the highway. Mr. Godfrey and Mr. Trainter are watching that end."

"Do they think the saboteurs will get possession of the truck and run it into the river near here?" asked Buddy.

"No, they aren't likely to do that. The spies want to get the electric instruments. So they may hijack the truck and, after disabling the trusted men on it, drive the truck to some secret place and take off the shipment.

"Or they may drive up in another truck, overpower the factory men and take off the shipment into the spies' truck. For either one of those contingences Mr. Trainter and Mr.

Godfrey are prepared. But there is a third possibility."

"What's that?" asked Buddy.

"The saboteurs may transfer the stuff from the truck to a motor boat and try to escape by river. That's why I'm here, to run down the spies in their motor boat."

"Golly!" exclaimed Tom. "Then there's likely to be a chase?"

"There may be," said Mr. Weston, drily. "And I hope I win."

"What do you want us to do?" asked Buddy.

"Well, if the hijacking is done by motor boat, I'll start in and chase. I may want you boys to take a message to that effect from me to the other G men—your friends."

"Oh, can't we come with you?" asked Buddy.

"I'm afraid not," said Mr. Weston. "It will be too dangerous."

"Aw, shucks!" exclaimed Tom.

"We're not afraid," said Harry.

"And we might be able to help you," added Buddy.

"I think there'll be nothing doing about letting you boys go," said Mr. Weston. "But now I'd better get out on the float to watch and listen. You boys can stand by. When I give you the word, cut away and look for either Mr. Trainter or Mr. Godfrey at their boarding places."

"They don't live in the same house," said Buddy.

"Yes, I know," commented Mr. Weston. "But get to one or the other. Now we'll just have to wait."

"How will you know the saboteur's motor boat if it comes along?" asked Buddy.

"There isn't likely to be more than one at this time of night," said Mr. Weston. "It will be a fast boat, and I have a description of it. I'll know it all right if it comes this way."

"Do you know what time?" asked Tom.

"Not exactly. But we know about the place, not far from here, where the switch, either to another truck or to the motor boat will be made. Mr. Godfrey or Mr. Trainter will be near there. They will fire two shots, followed by a third shot if the boat is to be used," said Mr. Weston. "If it's a truck there will be only two shots. Sort of like Paul Revere—'one if by land and two if by sea,' you know," and he smiled at the boys.

Buddy and his chums remembered the story of the midnight ride.

Then began a wait, rather a tedious one, for it lasted over an hour. Mr. Weston remained in his boat at the float, ready to cast off at the signal. The boys stayed in the shack, waiting.

Suddenly the silence of the night was broken by two shots—an interval—then another.

"They're coming by river!" exclaimed Mr. Weston. "I'll have to start the chase!"

CHAPTER XIII

BUDDY'S RIDE

THE three signal shots galvanized into action not only the G man but also Buddy and his chums. It is hardly necessary to add that Gosum also sprang up and barked. Then the setter looked at his master as if to apologize for breaking the silence imposed on him.

"It's all right, Gosum," said Buddy. "It's quite all right to bark now. I guess the spies know we're after 'em."

Gosum wagged his tail in appreciation of forgiveness, and then followed Buddy and the other boys out of the shack down to the float.

As they ran down, Buddy and his dog in the lead, Mr. Weston could be heard fumbling at the mooring lines.

"I'm going to cast off," he said to the boys in a low voice. "The spies' boat will be along any moment now and I don't want her to get too much of a lead."

"What do you want us to do?" asked Tom.

"Stay here until you see me taking after the other boat. Then hurry back to town and tell Mr. Godfrey or Mr. Trainter. You had better telephone them, but in a guarded way, so if any spies in either boarding house are listening, they won't know too much."

"I know," said Harry. "Like Buddy did before."

"Exactly. Hark! Isn't that a boat coming down the river?"

They all paused to listen, Mr. Weston had reached the stern mooring line which he was about to loosen.

"It's a boat all right," Buddy said.

"And coming fast," added Harry.

"Do you think it's the one you want?" asked Tom. "And do you think you can get her?" He had sized up the G man's motor boat. It was a sturdy craft, but none too speedy, Buddy's chums thought. And later events proved they were right.

"I think it's the boat I want," said Mr. Weston. "But whether I can overtake her, even if I get an even start from here, is a question. I'll jump in and start my motor. Can you cast off the stern line, Buddy?"

"Sure I can."

"Then do it when I give the word. Make it snappy!"

"Sure," said Buddy making his way along the float to the stern line of the G man's motor boat. Gosum was close to Buddy.

It was now darker than before, as heavier clouds were floating over the moon. But outside the shack, where the lights were glowing, Buddy and his chums could see dimly what was taking place.

Mr. Weston threw over the self starting lever and the motor caught at once and began throbbing. There was a clutch on the engine and it was necessary to put this in gear before the propeller would engage and move the boat.

The put-put of the approaching craft sounded louder now. It was, clearly, a fast and powerful boat. The pulses of Buddy and his chums tingled with excitement. Even Gosum seemed thrilled by what was about to happen, but he kept out of Buddy's way and did not so much as whimper.

"Better put out those lights in the shack," advised Mr. Weston. "They show me up too plainly. I can't hope to take up the chase without being seen or heard, but there's no use sticking myself right out in the glow. Put out the lights, will you, boys?"

"Sure," said Tom and he and Harry ran back to the shack, leaving Buddy on the float working at the knot of the stern line.

"Is it clear, Buddy?" asked Mr. Weston in a low voice. He was speeding the motor now and getting ready to let in the clutch which would start the propeller churning the water and send his boat away on the dark chase. "Cast me off, Buddy!" the G man called.

"The rope seems to be tangled," Buddy said.

"It shouldn't be," said Mr. Weston. "I made a slip knot so all you should have to do is to pull on the short end and it will be free. Give it a hard yank!"

"I will," said Buddy.

He leaned against the stern of the motorboat to brace himself. He glanced up at the shack. The last light went out.

"Quick, Buddy!" called Mr. Weston. "Here she comes!"

Buddy glanced across the river, toward the opposite shore, and up stream. Just then the moon showed for a moment through a rift in the clouds. And in the sudden gleam Buddy saw a long, low motor boat speeding down stream. Not a light showed aboard, nor was there any sound save the throbbing of the motor and the thresh of the propeller.

"Cast off!" implored Mr. Weston. "Hurry or I'll miss her!"

Buddy gave one last, hard tug at the rope. It loosed quickly—so quickly that he lost his balance. He thought he was going to topple off the float and into the water. But, instead, he fell backward upon the little stern deck of the G man's craft, the end of the mooring line still in his hand.

Buddy held fast to this for he knew if he dropped it the line would foul the now churning propeller. Mr. Weston had thrown in the clutch and his boat was rapidly moving away from the float, heading down stream and almost parallel with the spies' craft.

Buddy grunted a little as he fell aboard. A moment later he was aware that Gosum had leaped from the float and was crouching beside him. The moon was again obscured and it was quite dark.

"Good work, Buddy!" called Mr. Weston in a low voice. "You cast me off just in time."

"Yes," answered the red-haired lad as he sat up and grasped a rail to keep from going overboard, "I guess I did."

"What's that?" exclaimed Mr. Weston. "Are you aboard, Buddy?"

"I sure am, sir." was the reply. "But I couldn't help it. I lost my balance pulling loose the stern mooring line and I fell right here on the after deck."

"Well!" exclaimed the G man. "I didn't count on giving you a ride, Buddy. But I'm glad you fell aboard instead of overboard."

"So am I," chuckled the red-haired boy as he eased himself off the little after deck and down into the cockpit of the boat near the compartment which houses the motor. "And I'm glad I didn't get tangled in the line to be dragged after the boat. And I'm glad I kept hold of the line so it wouldn't foul your propeller."

"Good work all round, even if it was partly accident," said the G man. "What's that?" he added quickly. "Are your two chums with you?" For Mr. Weston heard noises other than those made by Buddy.

"It's my dog," was the answer. "He came aboard, too."

"Um!" murmured Mr. Weston. "I have more company than I counted on. Not that I mind," he hastily added, "but I didn't want to bring you into danger, Buddy."

"Is there danger, sir?"

"There may be. Those are desperate men and ruthless. I don't know what may happen if I manage to get close enough to order them to stop and let me make fast to them. I'm not going to let those valuable electric instruments fall into the hands of the Germans."

"How could that happen?" asked Buddy. "They can't ship anything to Germany from this country."

"I'll talk about that later," said Mr. Weston. "The thing to do now is to make sure you're safe. Come up forward and crouch down well below the bow, which, luckily is quite high. You'll be out of the reach of any possible bullets there. And bring your dog."

"Come on, Gosum," ordered Buddy in a low voice.

Boy and dog were soon in a protected place, crouching below the combing of the bow. The G man's boat was now gathering speed and threw a considerable spray.

Buddy took one quick observation over the gunwale. He saw the other craft forging ahead in the darkness. No light or sound came from her.

"Think you can catch 'em?" asked Buddy.

"I don't know," replied the G man. "It's a little too early in the chase. But I think their boat is much faster than mine. I'm getting about all the speed I can out of this tub, even with the current to help us. I had to commandeer this boat in a hurry. It isn't one I'd pick if I had my choice."

"They seem to be leaving us behind," Buddy ruefully commented.

"Seems so," admitted the G man.

"Do you think they have the stuff on board?"

"Hardly a doubt of it. Mr. Godfrey wouldn't have given the signals unless the saboteurs were trying to escape by boat with their loot."

"And I'm afraid they're going to escape," said Buddy. "They're farther off than ever."

"Yes, they are," admitted Mr. Weston. "Duck down!" he suddenly shouted.

There was a flash of fire from the other boat, followed by a sharp report. But before the noise of the shot reached the ears of Buddy and the G man there was the whine of a bullet in the air over their heads.

"Missed!" chuckled Mr. Weston. "Keep down, Buddy! I'm going to see if I can swing over closer to the rascals!"

CHAPTER XIV

MISSING

Tom and Harry, hastening from the float up to the shack to put out the lights, as Mr. Weston had requested, heard the G man's motor boat moving out into the river.

"I hope he gets those spies," remarked Tom.

"Same here," echoed Harry. "I wish we could have gone with Mr. Weston in the boat."

"So do I, and I guess Buddy wishes the same," said Tom.

They did not, of course, know that Buddy was having his wish fulfilled and was getting an unexpected ride with the G man.

Harry and Tom needed but a comparatively few seconds to put out the two lamps that were gleaming inside the shack. A lantern had been set outside the door.

"I guess we'd better put that out, too," suggested Tom.

"Sure," decided Harry. "I'll do it."

As he stepped out of the now darkened shack to extinguish the lantern, Harry heard some one walking toward the small building. It was now quite dark again. The moon was once more obscured. Harry could hear the sound of the G man's motor boat growing more and more faint as the craft moved away from the float and down the river. But above that noise was the echo of approaching footsteps.

"That you, Buddy?" asked Harry. He naturally supposed the red-haired boy would now be coming back from the float, after the casting off of the government man's craft.

There was no answer, but the approaching footsteps came to a quick and silent stop.

"What's the matter?" called Tom from within the shack.

"I thought I heard Buddy coming back," answered Tom, peering into the darkness. First he looked toward the river, which was in a lighter zone than that of the little forest glade on shore. For the sky was open above the river, and, in spite of the clouds, a faint gleam from the moon struggled through. But it was very dark on shore.

"Is Buddy there?" asked Tom, coming out to stand beside his chum.

"I thought so," answered Harry. "But he didn't answer me. Listen! Do you hear anything?"

The two boys froze into silence, standing on the little platform in front of the door of the shack. The put-put of the G man's motor boat was now scarcely audible.

Then, once more, came stealthy footsteps.

"Buddy!" called Harry. "Is that you?"

Once more silence. Once again a sudden stopping of the sound of footsteps.

"That's queer," said Harry in a low voice.

"Sure is," commented Tom in a whisper. "But did you notice where those footsteps came from?"

"Off there," replied Harry, pointing toward

the woods. Of course Tom could not see his chum's extended hand, but he guessed that Harry was pointing toward the trees.

"Yes, off toward the woods," spoke Tom in a whisper. "But Buddy wouldn't be coming from that direction. He would be coming back from the river. We left him on the float, helping Mr. Weston cast off."

"That's right," agreed Harry. "This must be somebody else."

"Come on inside the shack," urged Tom. "I don't like this. I think there's some funny business going on around here."

"But where's Buddy?" asked Harry.

"I don't know. Buddy wouldn't be coming out of the woods, unless he circled around, up and away from the float, and he wouldn't do that. He and Gosum would naturally come straight back here after Mr. Weston left."

"That's so," agreed Harry. "We haven't heard so much as a whimper out of the dog. Buddy wouldn't let him bark when there's secret government work like this going on. But Gosum would make some noise coming through the brush. And we haven't heard him."

"No—only those footsteps in the woods," said Tom in low tones. "And we don't hear them now—do we?" He and Harry froze into silence again but heard nothing—not even the put-put of the G man's craft.

"Come on—back in the shack," urged Tom and the two boys went in and closed the door, shooting the inside bolt.

Once inside, Tom and Harry felt more secure. At least they could not be suddenly attacked. But they were uneasy and apprehensive. Those stealthy footsteps were certainly not reassuring—especially when they knew their friends, the G men, were after the saboteurs.

If the two chums had expected their small castle, in the shape of the old fish shack, to be assaulted by the enemy, they were disappointed —agreeably so. For after they had remained inside, in the darkness for some time, scarcely daring to move about, and nothing had happened, Tom whispered:

"Are we going to stay here all night?"

"I hope not," responded Harry. "But isn't it queer Buddy doesn't come up from the float?"

"It sure is. Maybe he and Mr. Weston are having trouble getting the boat started."

"The boat left long ago."

"So it did. But where's Buddy?"

Harry couldn't answer that question. But he acted. Opening the door he called into the darkness: "Buddy, are you there?"

No answer, of course. Then, as he remembered the stealthy footsteps in the clump of trees and bushes, Harry called boldly: "Who are you and what do you want?"

Nor was there any reply to this hail. Then Harry decided on more decided action. Tom heard his chum fumbling with a match box which Harry had taken from his pocket.

"What are you going to do, Harry?" Tom asked.

"Strike a light and see what's going on. There's some mystery here and I don't like it for a cent. I'm afraid something has happened to Buddy and Mr. Weston."

"I don't see how that could be. If there was any rough-house going on down there at the float, we'd have heard it. It's only about 200 feet away. Besides, we heard the boat moving off."

"Yes, but why didn't Buddy come back?" asked Harry.

"Maybe we'd better go down to the float," suggested Tom.

"Just what I'm going to do," declared Harry. He struck a match, set one of the lamps aglow and then reached for the lantern.

"Better duck inside while you light that," said Tom.

"Why?"

"You'll be a good target, lighting a lantern

out there in the dark. Some of those saboteurs might take a shot at you—not to hit you, maybe, but to scare you."

"We've got to take a chance," decided Harry. "Here goes!"

He reached out, got the lantern and it was soon shedding its beams into the darkness. It was a silent darkness. Only the sound of the trees and bushes rustling in the wind could be heard.

"Come on," called Harry to Tom. "Let's go down to the float."

Somewhat apprehensive, yet resolute in their anxiety to rescue Buddy if he was in danger, the two boys walked down to the river. The lantern illuminated the path. When they reached the floating platform at which boats were moored, the moon suddenly came out brilliantly. It flooded the place with silvery light. It also served to show that the float was deserted.

"Buddy isn't here!" exclaimed Tom.

"By golly, the saboteurs got him!" gasped Harry. "Come on, we've got to notify the G men!"

The two boys started running.

CHAPTER XV

CAPTURED

THE echoes of the shot from the boat of the saboteurs, and the ugly whine of the bullet, over the heads of Buddy and Mr. Weston, had died away in the darkness.

"Keep down, Buddy! Keep down!" called the G man as he tried to inch a little bit more speed from his craft. "Keep down and keep Gosum down. They may fire again before I can close with them."

"I'll keep down," agreed Buddy as he snuggled beneath the high gunwhale and bow of the boat. "Quiet, Gosum," he softly ordered the setter. And the intelligent dog became silent, ceasing the whimper and low growl that had followed the shot.

In the uncertain and intermittent light of the moon in the clouded sky, Mr. Weston could see that he was now gaining slightly on the other boat. The chase was now almost parallel, the two craft being about 100 feet apart. It was not light enough for Mr. Weston to make out any occupants of the saboteurs' boat. He had no doubt but that several desperate men were aboard, trying to flee with the valuable electric instruments they had hijacked from the factory truck. Buddy did not understand how, after having stolen the instruments, the saboteurs and spies could get them to Germany, where they were much needed.

Later Mr. Weston said it was comparatively easy for the spies to make contact with other spies who, posing as neutrals, could go openly to Argentine, which was then the only South American country maintaining friendly relations with the Axis.

From Argentine the valuable instruments could be shipped aboard a submarine to Germany and there used against the United Nations.

But just now Buddy was more concerned

with what the result of the G man's pursuit of the spies' craft would be. Could Mr. Weston overtake the other boat and either force it ashore, or compel the men to surrender.

"It's a big job for one G man," mused Buddy. "I wish I could help him." But he realized this was out of the question. He was more of a liability than an asset, just at present. He hadn't intended to come on this trip, but was there by an accident and chance. He must make the best of it.

"Keep low, Buddy," advised Mr. Weston in a tense voice. "I think I'm going to close in."

By what skill of navigation, or by what reserve power in the G man's boat, it was brought about, Buddy didn't know.

But a moment later Mr. Weston had put his craft close alongside the fleeing boat, and, holding the wheel with his left hand, the G man drew his automatic in his right hand and called:

"Reach for the sky or I'll shoot!"

The moon showed for an instant, enabling

Buddy to see Mr. Weston covering several figures crouched low in the boat which had been overtaken. Buddy fully expected to hear a fusillade of shots from the hijackers. But something more unexpected and dramatic happened.

There was a sound from the rear of Mr. Weston's boat—the sound of another and very swift craft approaching. For a moment Buddy hoped it might be Mr. Godfrey and Mr. Trainter who had come to the aid of their comrade G man.

But a moment later he knew it was reinforcements from the camp of the enemy.

The second boat of the saboteurs which had approached at fast speed on the port side of Mr. Weston's boat (his starboard side being now up against the first boat) now went into bereverse. The G man's boat was now caught between the two enemy craft.

"Let him have it!" some one in the second saboteur boat snarled.

Buddy looked up in time to see a tall man

reach over and hit Mr. Weston on the head with a club. The G man dropped to the cockpit of his boat.

"That settles him!" growled the saboteur who had given the order to strike down the G man. "Keep going, you fellows," he ordered those in the first boat. "We'll take care of this G man."

"Guess he won't need much taking care of," chuckled the fellow who had dealt the blow. "I got him right on the noodle!"

Indeed, as Buddy noted from the limp manner in which Mr. Weston had slumped down, there was no fight left in the G man.

The three boats, momentarily, had formed a little flotilla and were keeping on down the river. Mr. Weston had not had time to throw a grappling line aboard the first boat. It was an easy matter, then, for the first boat to veer to one side and keep on going down the stream. Buddy wondered what was going to happen to him and to Mr. Weston, and, also, to Gosum.

The clever setter, following the training Buddy had given him, had maintained silence except for low growls.

For a short time the second, speedy boat of the spies had kept in contact with Mr. Weston's craft. Buddy, taking a careful observation above the gunwhale, noted that two men had grasped the metal railing which ran around the edge of the gunwale, thus holding the two craft together as the engines of both were still operating in forward.

"What'll we do with this boat?" some one inquired from the crew of saboteurs.

"And the G man?" asked another.

"We'll take the boat to our dock and tie her up," decided the leader who had given the orders to strike down Mr. Weston. "It's an old tub, but maybe we can paint her up, give her another name and number, and use her. Shut off her engine, somebody, and we'll take her in tow."

"What'll we do with him?" asked a voice

as the speaker prepared to board the insensible G man's craft.

"Dump him overboard for all I care," growled the leader.

"It might be dangerous," some one suggested.

"Then leave him aboard and we'll hide him away. But truss him up and gag him. He may come out of his sleep and make trouble."

"He'll sleep until morning," chuckled the wielder of the club that had felled Mr. Weston.

"So much the better. Well, get aboard, somebody, shut off that motor and make the boat fast to our stern."

Cowering amid a pile of tarpaulins in the bottom of the boat, which pieces evidently were used as coverings for the engine in wet weather, Buddy could see several men getting aboard the G man's boat from the capturing craft. One reached over and cut the ignition switch of the motor. The boat was now being taken along by the movement of the spies' craft, several members of that crew still holding the two together.

"Shut off your motor, Jule," some one called—evidently one of those forming a human grapple. "We can't hold on much longer."

"All right. Cut her off," assented the leader. "Then rig a tow line. But first truss up that G man."

It was when some of the crew started in on this work that Buddy and his dog was discovered.

"Say, chief!" cried one of the trussing gang, "there's a boy here!"

"A boy?" was the surprised exclamation.

"Yes, and a dog!" added another of the captors.

"Jumping junipers!" gasped the leader. "What's the game?"

"Hanged if I know," said one of the men now in the G man's boat. "But here they are—a boy and a dog."

Buddy blinked as the rays of a flashlight were suddenly focused on him and Gosum as they huddled together, crouched on the floor of the cockpit. The setter growled omniously.

"Quiet, Gosum!" said Buddy in a low voice and Gosum subsided.

"Who are you?" demanded the man who, evidently went by the name 'Jule.' He leered at Buddy from the other boat. The two craft were now drifting down the river together. "Who are you?"

"Nobody you know," said Buddy as coolly as he could.

"Oh, smart kid, eh?" sneered Jule.

"Shall I smack him down?" growled one of the crew.

Jule hesitated. Buddy's fate seemed to hang in the balance.

Finally, after what seemed a long time but which, really, was only a few seconds, Jule growled:

"No. We'll have to hide him away, too."

"And the dog?"

"Yes. The dog. I might keep him for myself. But tie the boy up and gag him, too. We can't take any chances of him yelling for help when we go ashore."

"I won't yell," said Buddy, trying not to let his voice tremble. "But you'd better let me go and also Mr.—"

He paused before uttering Mr. Weston's name. He realized that the G men liked to remain anonymous.

"Who's your friend?" demanded Jule.

"Try and guess," said Buddy. "But he knows who you are."

"He don't know nothin' now," sneered the man who had struck down the G man. "And he won't for a long time."

"Enough talk!" snapped the leader. "Tie 'em up. Start towing this boat and we'll head for the cove. Lively now! No telling when some more of these nosey G men may come along."

Buddy realized it was useless to fight against such odds. In a short time he was tied fast, a handkerchief was placed over his mouth in such a fashion he could not cry out, and then he and Mr. Weston, both captives, were laid out in the bottom of the boat.

A little later Buddy could tell, by the motion, that the craft in which he and the G man were prisoners, was being towed down the river.

CHAPTER XVI

LEFT ALONE

TOM and Harry knew where Mr. Godfrey and Mr. Trainter boarded in town. With Buddy they had often discussed the necessity of, some day, having to take a message to either G man.

"But if you call to see us, or if you telephone," Mr. Godfrey had instructed Buddy and his chums, "don't blurt out what you may have to tell us. Don't ask questions or say anything that will give away our secret. At our boarding places we are not known to be G men. We are just workmen in the electric factory."

Now, as the two boys were hurrying away from the shack, with the knowledge that Buddy had mysteriously disappeared from the float, about the same time the boat of Mr. Weston had cast off, this cautionary advice recurred to them.

"Do you think we ought to tell Mr. Godfrey

first, or Mr. Trainter?" asked Tom as he jogged along beside his chum.

"Neither one," replied Harry quickly.

"Why not? We've got to find Buddy."

"Sure, but don't you remember what Mr. Godfrey said about not telling anything out in the open? We've got to let the G men know what has happened, but we've got to be secret about it."

"You mean we've got to tell them in the strip and stick code?" asked Tom.

"No; but we don't want to blurt it out either at their boarding places or over the telephone. We've got to be secret about it. Anyhow, I don't believe it would do any good to go to the boarding places now."

"Why not?"

"Because, Tom," said Harry, "neither Mr. Godfrey nor Mr. Trainter would be back there yet. They went in cars to try to catch the saboteurs on the road. Then the spies changed to a boat and Mr. Weston went after them in his boat."

"And maybe he took Buddy along," suggested Tom, hopefully.

"Maybe he did, but I don't believe so. It would be too dangerous for Buddy. But, anyhow, I don't believe the other two G men would be back in town yet."

"Then what shall we do?" Tom wanted to know.

"We'll go tell Buddy's father, first," decided Harry. "He ought to know, and he can tell us best what to do next. If Buddy has been kidnapped, the police as well as the F.B.I. ought to know."

"Sure!" assented Tom. "But I don't believe Buddy would let himself be kidnapped without putting up a holler. And we didn't hear him yell."

"No, we didn't. Which sort of makes it look as if Mr. Weston, at the last minute, invited Buddy into the boat."

"I hope so. But it doesn't seem reasonable," said Tom. "Anyhow, you think it's best to go to Buddy's house first?"

"I sure do."

Tom and Harry headed for the home of their red-haired chum. Mr. and Mrs. Martyne were both up, reading, for the hour was not late.

"What's the matter, boys?" asked Mr. Martyne as he admitted Tom and Harry. He could tell, by their startled looks, that something had happened, and he quickly asked: "Where's Buddy?"

"Something—something has happened," gasped Tom.

"Buddy is—he's gone," gulped Harry.

"Don't tell me Buddy is—is—" faltered Mrs. Martyne as she came out into the hall where Mr. Martyne was now standing with the two boys.

"He just disappeared from the float when Mr. Weston went away in his motor boat," explained Harry. "So did Gosum."

"But he didn't fall in," said Tom quickly.

"We didn't hear any splash. And, anyhow, Buddy can swim like a fish."

"And Gosum didn't bark," added Harry.

"Oh, well, then I guess it can't be serious," said Mr. Martyne. His wife looked much relieved. Buddy's father added: "I think Buddy was invited, at the last moment, to accompany Mr. Weston."

"I hope so," said Tom, and Harry echoed that wish.

"The first thing to do, however," decided Mr. Martyne, "is to go down to the shack and make a search. Maybe the footsteps you heard in the woods were Buddy's."

"But he didn't answer when we called," objected Tom.

"He may have had a reason for keeping quiet," said Mr. Martyne. "Then he wouldn't answer. But we'll go to the shack and then we'll let the G men know. You boys had better tell your folks that you are here."

Harry and Tom telephoned their homes. Their parents were surprised and somewhat alarmed about Buddy. Mr. Martyne said he thought there was no real danger, with the G men ready and anxious to assist in the search for the missing red-haired lad.

"And we're going to help catch the saboteurs," concluded Tom in his last words telephoned to his home.

"We sure are," echoed Harry.

Then, not without many cautions from Mrs. Martyne, her husband and the two boys started for the river shack. It was still dark, because of the often cloud-obscured moon, and a storm seemed in the making.

"But it isn't so late," said Mr. Martyne, looking at his watch by the fitful gleam of the moon.

"What time is it?" asked Tom.

"Not yet 10," answered Buddy's father.

The three were soon at the shack. But it

needed only a quick search, in and about, to disclose that Buddy was not there.

"Gosum is gone, too," said Tom.

"Naturally," said Harry. "You wouldn't catch Buddy's dog leaving him."

"I'm glad Buddy has his dog," said Mr. Martyne. "Well, there is nothing to be gained by staying here. As far as I can see," he went on, playing over the float the beams of a flash-light he carried, "Buddy didn't fall in. There is no water splashed on the float as there would have been if Buddy had tumbled in. Now we'll go tell the G men."

Meanwhile Buddy was being carried into captivity. It was not a long voyage down the river in the towed craft where he was tied and gagged and where Mr. Weston was an unconscious prisoner.

Before Buddy had time to feel very uncomfortable from his bonds and the handkerchief tied over his nose and mouth, he sensed that the towing craft was slowing speed. The towed boat, in which he and Mr. Weston were guarded by some of the gang, kept on moving.

"Fend us off!" called one of the men in the towed craft. "We'll ram you if you don't."

"All right," answered some one from the bigger boat. "We're going to tie up here."

The two boats, as Buddy could tell by the sounds and motions, were soon made fast to some sort of dock or float, just which he could not determine. He was stretched on some bags and tarpaulins in the bottom of the boat in which he had so accidentally set out with Mr. Weston. The G man, still unconscious from the blow, was near Buddy. Also crouched near the red-haired lad was Gosum. Buddy tried to reach out a hand to touch the setter, but was too tightly bound.

However, Gosum seemed to sense what Buddy meant, and the dog's tail could be heard gently thumping against the bottom boards.

"What are we going to do with these two

birds?" asked one of the men in the boat with Buddy. "Leave 'em here?"

"Of course not," answered some one, whose voice Buddy recognized as that of Jule, the leader. "Has the G man moved?"

"Not an inch, boss."

"Then you'll have to carry him up to the house."

"What about the boy?"

"He can walk if you take off some of the ropes. But tell him if he tries any tricks they'll be his last."

"I guess he heard you, boss," chuckled one of Buddy's captors.

Indeed the red-haired boy had heard and resolved to submit quietly, at least for a time. But he was plotting to escape and save Mr. Weston.

Buddy felt hands fumbling in the darkness at the ropes that bound his ankles. His feet were soon free.

"Stand up and walk," roughly ordered one

of the men. "And no monkey business; you hear?"

Buddy heard but he couldn't answer because of the gag. He stood up, trying in vain in the gloom, to get a glimpse of the faces of his captors. But the dark clouds favored them. Buddy saw two men lift the limp form of Mr. Weston out of the boat.

"Here's an old door," said some one on what, as Buddy could now see, was a dock at which the two boats were tied. "We can lay him on that and carry him up to the house."

"So," mused Buddy, "we are going to be held prisoners in a house. Probably a hide-out for the spy gang."

"Come on, kid!" one of Buddy's captors ordered. And then he seemed surprised as he called: "Hey, what about the kid's dog, boss?"

"Let him come along. If we turn him loose he might find his way back and give the game away. Lock the boy and dog up together."

"Come on, kid. And you, too, dog!" ordered

the man. Buddy felt himself half pulled, half led, out of the boat, onto the dock and up a path at the end of which he could dimly see, in the darkness, a large house. Gosum followed, silent but, doubtless, wondering what it was all about. Buddy heard the men stumbling along with the old door on which lay the unconscious G man.

"We sure are up against it," mused Buddy as he followed in custody of the man who had hold of him.

Some one farther up the path was leading the way with a lantern. Buddy could see the bobbing light and the long, grotesque shadows cast by his legs.

The man with the lantern mounted some steps and then Buddy could see him opening a door in the old house. It was a big one, as Buddy noticed when the moon came out briefly. It was what might be called a mansion, and it was, evidently, being used as a headquarters by the gang of spies and saboteurs. Buddy knew there were many old and deserted mansions about Mountchester. He wondered which one this was and just where it was located.

"If I could only get my bearings, and find out just which this old house is," mused Buddy, "and if I could get some word back to Tom and Harry, they might let the G men know and we'd be rescued. But I don't know this place."

"Come on, kid!" sharply ordered the man as Buddy was hanging back, trying to see if he could identify anything about the house.

Buddy stepped forward. The ropes on his wrists were now beginning to pain him and the gag was most uncomfortable. Gosum followed.

Then a bit of luck came Buddy's way. The moon shone brilliantly for a moment. It reflected on the glass windows of a sort of cupola, or tower, on top of the big mansion. Buddy was thrilled.

"Now I know where I am!" he exulted.

A few minutes later he was led into the old house. He was thrust into a small room after the ropes had been taken from his wrists and the gag from his mouth. Gosum was pushed into the room with Buddy.

Then the door was locked.

Buddy and his dog were left alone.

CHAPTER XVII

CAPTIVITY

THINKING it best to telephone instead of going in person with Harry and Tom to seek Mr. Godfrey and Mr. Trainter, Buddy's father stopped in the first place he came to that had a public booth, after the three had left the river shack.

Mr. Martyne first called Mr. Godfrey, making his voice sound casual as he telephoned the G man's boarding house. But Mr. Godfrey wasn't it. There was better luck when he was connected with Mr. Trainter.

"Something has happened," said Mr. Martyne when he heard the G man's voice. "Red has disappeared."

"Oh, is that so," said Mr. Trainter, also casually in order to deceive any spies who might be listening. "Well, he'll be back. I'll be with you soon."

That was all, but it was enough to let Mr. Martyne know the G man would soon call at the house. "Red," was the name Buddy was frequently called. His father hoped Mr. Trainter would understand, as, indeed, he did.

Mr. Martyne and the two boys were soon back at Buddy's home.

"Any news?" asked Mrs. Martyne, and there was a catch in her voice as she tried to keep back the tears in her eyes.

"Not yet," said her husband. "But the G men will soon be here."

A little later Mr. Trainter and Mr. Godfrey both arrived, somewhat excited but not unduly alarmed.

"The saboteurs slipped away from us with the truck of electric things they took from the factory," said Mr. Godfrey. "We knew they were going to transfer to a boat so we gave Mr. Weston the signal."

"He got it," said Tom. "And he started off in his boat."

"And that was the last we saw of him or Buddy," said Harry.

"We'll find 'em both, and we'll round up the gang," declared Mr. Godfrey.

"We've got to have help, though," said Mr. Trainter. "I'll put in a call for more of our men. You stay here and get all the particulars from Tom and Harry," he said to Mr. Godfrey.

The night slowly passed. It was several hours before enough extra G men could be summoned from distant headquarters to come to Mountchester to solve not only the mystery of the stolen goods but also the disappearance of Buddy and Mr. Weston.

"For Mr. Weston and Buddy both seem to have fallen into the hands of the spies," said Mr. Godfrey when, finally, more G man arrived at Mr. Martyne's home.

Tom and Harry had been sent to their homes to get some rest before the activities that would start in the morning.

Mrs. Martyne, worn and anxious, was persuaded to go to bed, but she did not sleep much. Mr. Martyne remained up with the G men making plans to be carried out when daylight should come.

Buddy, too, a prisoner in the deserted mansion, spent a lonely and anxious night.

About an hour after he and Gosum had been thrust into the room, which was in darkness, the door opened and a man came in carrying a lantern. He also had some packages in one hand.

"Here's some grub for you and the dog," the man said. "I'm not anyone to let a dog go hungry, let alone a kid. Here's some sandwiches for you and the dog."

"Thanks," said Buddy. "But could I have a drink? I guess Gosum is thirsty, too."

"Who's Gosum?" asked the man.

"My dog."

"Oh! A queer name. Well, here's where you can get a drink." Going over to another door in the room, which Buddy had not seen before in the darkness, the man opened it. There was a small toilet room with a wash basin and water. "It's only cold water," said the man turning a faucet and thus proving his point. "The hot water is off for the duration," he chuckled. "You won't go thirsty, you nor the dog. And when this grub is gone I'll bring you more."

"How long are you going to keep me here?" asked Buddy.

"Not knowing, can't say. It's up to the boss and he won't tell."

"Do you mean Jule?" asked Buddy boldly.

"Hey! Lay off that!" sternly commanded the guard. "No names around here! It isn't healthy to use names; get that and let it sink in! Now don't try any tricks. You're going to stay here a while, but you won't die of thirst or hunger. And you can't get out, either!"

He added this as he caught sight of Buddy looking toward the only window in the room.

There was none in the small room where the wash basin was now gurgling with the sound of running water—only a small skylight high up in the ceiling. And now Buddy saw, as the man walked over to the window with his lantern, that it was protected by heavy iron bars.

There would be no escape from that; nor by the door, for Buddy could tell by the way it was shut that it was heavy. And the lock was also heavy and strong. He noted this as the man went out and prepared to turn the key on the outer side.

"Won't you leave me the lantern?" asked Buddy as he saw the man taking it away with him. And all the time the guard carried the lantern he held it in such a way that the rays never reflected on his face. Buddy could not see his features.

"Leave you the lantern, and have you signalling? I should say not," snarled the jailer. "You can find the way to your mouth in the dark, I guess. Anyhow, you'll have to."

He tramped out, leaving Buddy and Gosum alone again and in the darkness. But Buddy would not have been the boy he was if he had not a few matches with him. He now lighted one of these and found, on the floor of the room, a few splinters of wood. From one of these he made a little torch, sticking it in a crack beneath the wash basin so it would not shine through the skylight. By this little illumination Buddy could see to open the packages of food the man had left. There were some cheese and ham sandwiches and a few cookies.

By his little torch Buddy found in a closet in the toilet room a glass and a small tin basin. Into the basin he let run some water that Gosum lapped up eagerly. Then, having taken a drink himself, Buddy ate and gave the setter some of the bread and meat.

Gosum swallowed the food eagerly. Evidently the captivity was not worrying him much as long as Buddy was with him. Buddy, too, found he had more appetite than he had supposed at first.

"I must eat to keep up my strength," he told himself. "I've got to find a way out of here to save Mr. Weston. He may die if a doctor doesn't take care of him.

"But, anyhow, Gosum," exulted Buddy as he ate and drank, "I know where we are being held captives, and that's a good start."

For when Buddy had seen, in that quick glimpse as the moon shone through the clouds, the cupola on the house he recognized the old mansion.

It was known in and about Mountchester as the "Tower House." It had been built, many years ago, by a rich, eccentric man who had two hobbies. One was astronomy and the other astrology. The two, somehow, seemed to go together, according to this man, but astronomers are not agreed that the sun, moon and planets have any such power as astrologers give them.

For his astronomy hobby this man had built a sort of tower, or observatory, on the top of his house. From there he surveyed the stars and moon at night through a powerful telescope. During the day he poured over astrologic divinations and tried to sell his ideas to his neighbors.

So the rumor got around that the man was "queer," and, after his death, the house was said to be "haunted." The place was deserted. The furniture, or most of it, was taken away and relatives claimed it and the telescope. The "Tower House" became deserted and lonely and was seldom visited.

More than once Buddy and his chums had passed it but they had never been interested enough to go inside.

So, though Buddy recognized the place of his captivity by the tower, he was unaquainted with the interior. All he knew now was that he was locked in a room with his dog. He had food and water. He walked to the barred window. He found he could raise the sash, but the outside bars were strong and firmly in place. And they were too close together to permit of Buddy squeezing through.

Now the moon came out brighter. Buddy extinguished his little splinter torch. The moon disclosed, what Buddy had not noticed before, that in the room was a couch, a table and some chairs. Also on the couch were some old window drapes.

"I can make up a bed here," mused Buddy. "I can cover up and there'll be enough of the drapes to make a bed for Gosum. Here, boy!" he called his dog.

The dog came close to his red-haired master. Then Buddy made up a bed for himself and for his dog. Gosum was soon asleep—at least he was quiet. Buddy, tired and worried as he was, found sleep a little longer coming to him.

But at last he slumbered. How long he slept he did not know. But he was awakened by a noise at the door. Gosum leaped up, growled and barked. The key turned in the lock.

CHAPTER XVIII

THE CIPHER MESSAGE

Buddy sprang from the couch in some alarm. Gosum continued to bark and growl as he seemed about to spring at a man who entered the prison room.

Buddy, however, caught his setter by the collar and held him tight, saying:

"Down, Gosum! Quiet, boy!"

The dog grew quiet and the man, whose voice Buddy recognized as the same as the one of the night before, said:

"No call to get excited. I just brought you some breakfast."

"Oh," said Buddy, who was less excited than he had been when so suddenly awakened from sleep. "Well, after breakfast are you going to let us go?"

"Not much chance of that!" the man said. "Better not ask too many questions. Keep still and you won't be hurt. Here's some more grub for you and the dog. Will he bite?"

"Not his friends," said Buddy significantly.

"Well, I'm his friend. I like dogs. Here's some extra meat for you," and he tossed a bone to Gosum who, before he picked it up to take to a distant corner, wagged his tail in at least half a friendly signal.

"See he knows I like dogs," went on the man. "And here's a bottle of milk for you, with some more sandwiches."

"Well—thanks," said Buddy. It was the least he could say.

"And, mind you, no tricks!" warned the man in more surly tones as he went out of the room, locking the door.

Gosum did not even look up. The setter was busy with the bone. Buddy washed his hands and face, the cold water refreshing him. He had to dry on a handkerchief. Luckily he had a "spare," and he hung the damp handkerchief over a chair to dry as he ate his breakfast.

And then, with the daylight, and with a more substantial meal than he had made the night before, Buddy felt his courage coming back to him. He began to plot and plan.

He reviewed the events of the night before. He had no doubt but that Mr. Weston was also a captive, but in a different part of the Tower House. Buddy listened at the door, after he had eaten and when Gosum was stretched out beneath the window, content after his bone. But all the sounds Buddy could hear were such distant ones that they had no meaning for him.

"I know where I am," the red-haired boy reasoned. "If I could only let my folks and the G men, and Tom and Harry know I'm here, in the Tower House, they'd soon come to the rescue."

Buddy now began a closer examination of his prison than was possible in the darkness. Plenty of light came in through the iron-barred window. Buddy raised the sash to let in fresh air. He also carefully examined the bars. To his delight one was slightly loose at the lower end, where it fitted into a cross bar at the window still.

"If I had a stick to use for a lever, I think I could pry this bar loose," Buddy mused. "But even then, there isn't room for me to get out," he thought despondently. "The bars are too close together even with one pushed out."

Then he looked toward Gosum who had gone to sleep. A brilliant idea flashed through Buddy's mind.

"If I pried that bar loose, there would be room for Gosum to get out!" he murmured. "And if he could get out, he might go home, if I told him to—and when he gets to my house—wait—I could send a cipher message in Gosum's collar. It's a double collar. Only my friends know a strip of paper could be hidden in the collar.

"But," exclaimed Buddy, talking in whispers to himself now, "even if any of the spies stop Gosum, and find the message in between the two leather layers of his collar, they can't read it. For I'll send a cipher message! Then I'll let Gosum out between the bars and tell him to go home.

"I think I can beat the spies yet!"

There were two things for Buddy to do. One was to make a space between the bars large enough for Gosum to slip through. The other problem was to make and write a cipher message.

The prying out of the bar proved comparatively easy. Buddy found that one of the table legs was loose. He pulled it off, after some effort, and pushed the table against the wall so it would not topple over, standing on only three legs.

With the table leg, which was a substantial piece of wood, Buddy found he could push the loose bar outward. He did this, and then pulled it back into place so it would not be noticed by his guard.

"No use putting Gosum out until I can put

the cipher message in his collar," reasoned Buddy. "And that isn't going to be so easy. But it has to be done."

He began a more careful inspection of his prison. There were some odds and ends in one corner, a pile of rubbish, old boxes and broken bits of furniture.

Buddy exclaimed:

"Eureka!"

Which as everybody knows, means:

"I have found it!"

What Buddy had found was a discarded white window shade on a wooden roller.

"Now I can make the strip and stick cipher," said the red-haired lad. He felt so jubilant that he jumped up and clicked his heels together three times. This proceeding somewhat disturbed Gosum. But the setter dozed off again.

"You'll soon be on your way," said Buddy. "But I'm not going to start you off until after dark. There may be guards outside this old

Tower House and if they saw Gosum making for home they might stop him. I'll wait until it's dark. Then, Gosum, I'll pry out the bar, put you through the opening with the cipher in your collar, and we'll see what happens."

Buddy now had something to do which kept him from brooding on his rather dangerous position. He wondered what had happened to Mr. Weston but there was no way of learning.

Buddy's first object was to get a strip of the old, white window curtain that would approximate the strip of paper he and his chums used for their cipher. It was easy enough to pull the curtain from the roller and with his knife to cut a long strip, about an inch wide. This was the width Buddy and his chums used.

With a small saw-blade in his Boy Scout knife, Buddy next cut off a piece of the window shade roller about 15 inches long. He had to guess at this and also to guess at the size of the roller. But he took a chance on it being about an inch in diameter, which was the size he, Tom and Harry had fixed on. Most ordinary shade rollers are this size.

Buddy did not do this all at once. He had to be prepared for one of the men unexpectedly entering his prison room. He did not want to be caught in the act of making a cipher.

So it was well along in the afternoon, and about an hour from the time the man had brought his lunch, that Buddy had the cipher finished.

He had rolled the curtain strip about the piece of stick and had then printed, vertically the message. It was simple:

IN TOWER HOUSE

Unwinding the lapping strip from the stick, Buddy, with the stump of pencil he luckily had in a pocket, began to fill in extra letters which made, to those not in the secret, a mere jumble of meaningless words which might have been Greek. But when the strip was taken from Gosum's collar, and wound on another stick, such as Tom or Harry or the G men had, the message would stand out in a straight up and down line. All the other letters, even if they fell in a straight line, would mean nothing.

Buddy tested his cipher carefully as dusk began to fall. It was as perfect as he could make it. He hoped his friends would be able to translate it.

"But I'm pretty sure they will," he mused.

Looking at the straight strip of window curtain, all the casual observer would see was a jumble of letters starting off with:

SIXOPAXNPTXKP

But when the strip was wound about the stick, spiral fashion, the laps joined closely, Buddy's message stood out:

IN TOWER HOUSE.

"Tom and Harry will know what that means," Buddy reasoned. "They can tell the

G men. And now, Gosum, I think it's about time you started."

Buddy slipped the strip of paper into the secret compartment of his dog's collar. He tossed the stick back on the rubbish heap. It would not be needed, for Tom, Harry or the G men would use their own stick.

Buddy waited until the man had brought his supper, went out and locked the door. Waiting until it was quite dark, Buddy pried the loose bar out and raised Gosum's forefeet to the sill.

"Go home, old boy! Go home! Home, Gosum!" Buddy ordered.

The setter paused and whined. He did not want to leave his master.

"You must go home to save me and the G man. Take the secret cipher home, Gosum!" said Buddy in his dog's ears. "Go on! Home!"

With a last look, as if protesting but obeying, the setter managed to wiggle out through the opening in the bars. It was but a short distance to the ground. Buddy had a glimpse of his dog pausing once to look back in the dim light of the moon that had not yet fully risen.

"Home, Gosum!" Buddy called softly. "Home!"

CHAPTER XIX

THE SECRET TUNNEL

BUDDY, standing at the barred window, which he had opened enough to let out his dog, watched the setter. Gosum was in two minds, whether to obey his master, and go to the home in Mountchester, or whether to return to share Buddy's captivity.

The captive dared not call out again to order his dog home. Gosum was so far away in the woods, now, that Buddy would have had to raise his voice and this might be heard by the spies in the old Tower House.

But the moon, for a moment once more, shining brightly, Buddy motioned with his hand in the direction of his home, pointing to it and waving Gosum on. Then, with a somewhat sorrowful wag of his tail, the dog trotted away and was lost to sight in the dark patch of trees.

"I hope he makes it," mused Buddy. "I hope he gets home and that my father, or some of the G men, or Tom or Harry will think to look in Gosum's collar. If they do, I know they'll rescue me."

As Buddy worked to bend back in place the iron bar he had pushed outward to let his dog slip through, the red-haired boy knew there were many chances against his plan.

"These spies may have the place surrounded," Buddy reasoned. "They may catch Gosum. If they do, I hope they don't harm him. I don't believe they'll catch on to the secret, double collar. But, even if they do, I don't believe they can read my cipher message.

"Oh, if Gosum can only make it, I'll be rescued!"

There were other chances against him, as Buddy well knew. Gosum had strayed away from his former home and had come to the fish shack, where Buddy claimed him. The dog once more might become a wanderer, since Buddy had ordered him away.

"But I've got to take those chances," Buddy reasoned. "The G men take chances and I must do the same. There! The bar's back in place. Unless they look at it closely, they'll never know I pushed it out. But I wonder what they'll say when the guard comes in the morning to bring my breakfast, and sees Gosum gone? Well, I'll have to say he got away—which is true enough. I'll wait until morning to see what happens. But I hope they come to rescue me tonight. It isn't too late."

Buddy had to judge the time by the moon, as he had no watch. But, being a Boy Scout, he could pretty well calculate the hour by the position of the moon in the sky overhead. He judged it to be about 11 o'clock.

"Well, there's nothing more I can do now," Buddy mused. "I may as well go to bed."

He curled up on the couch, pulling the coverings over him. He looked at the place where Gosum had made his bed on some old bags. In spite of himself, Buddy felt a lump come into his throat and there was a suspicious moisture in his eyes as he thought of his dog. But he took a grip on his feelings and exclaimed:

"Cut it out, cry baby!"

Buddy felt better after that. He did not fall asleep at once. He heard the sounds of voices and footsteps, distantly, in the old mansion. He wondered whether Gosum had been discovered and intercepted. Then, almost in spite of himself, Buddy fell asleep.

Meanwhile, back in Buddy's home, there was, at this same time, a council of war being held. Mr. Martyne had summoned the parents of Tom and Harry and there were several G men, who had been called from nearby places by Mr. Trainter and Mr. Godfrey.

"We've got to do something about this," Mr. Godfrey exclaimed. "Those spies have captured Buddy and Mr. Weston. We've got to rescue them. And we've got to do it tonight!"

"We aren't quite ready to crack down on

the gang of saboteurs who have been taking things from the electric factory," said Mr. Trainter. "We need to close up some loop holes and then we'll get the whole gang."

"We can't wait for that," said Mr. Godfrey. "This is an emergency and we must act tonight. If we only knew the hide-out of the gang we could go there in force. They probably have Buddy and Mr. Weston hidden there. But where is the hideout?"

"We know one place," said Mr. Trainter. "That's near where they switched from trucks to the motor boat."

"There's nothing there now," said another G man who was working on the case. "Larry and I searched there just before we came here."

"Then we'll just have to scatter and try to pick up some leads," decided Mr. Trainter.

"But I did want to start to rescue Buddy and Mr. Weston tonight!" exclaimed Mr. Godfrey. "Tomorrow may—"

He was going to say "too late," but a glimpse of the face of Buddy's mother, in an adjoining room, stopped him and he changed it to the phrase:

"Tomorrow we may get on their trail."

There was a little more talk. The G men were assuring the worried parents that the gang would be afraid to harm Buddy, when, suddenly, Lola Wagg, the Martyne maid, came into the conference room.

"Excuse me," she said, "but there's a dog scratching and whining at the kitchen door. I'm afraid to open it."

"A dog?" exclaimed Mr. Martyne.

"Yes, sir, it whines like a dog and it barks like a dog. But I'm afraid—"

Followed by Tom and Harry, Mr. Martyne made a dash for the kitchen. He flung open the door and in came Gosum. The dog was covered with briars, brambles and stickers. He was muddy and dirty, but he wagged his tail as if to say:

"I made it!"

"It's Buddy's dog!" exclaimed Tom.

"Then Buddy ought to be here, too," said Harry.

Mr. Martyne stepped out on the back porch and called:

"Buddy! Buddy!"

There was no answer, but Gosum barked as if to say:

"I'm here. I just came from Buddy. Can't you understand?"

Tom did, a moment later, for he exclaimed:

"I get it! Buddy is being held a prisoner by the spies and he sent his dog to tell us."

"That's right!" echoed Harry. "Buddy has trained Gosum to come home when he sends him. That's what Buddy did now. He sent Gosum home and Gosum came."

"It's too bad he can't talk," said one of the G men. "If he could speak he might tell us where Buddy is held captive."

"But he can talk!" cried Tom. "Look in

the collar! The double collar! Buddy planned it with us that if anything ever happened to him or us, and Gosum was with us, he'd send him back with a message; a cipher message."

"That's right!" exclaimed Harry. "Let's look in the collar."

Gosum wagged his tail joyfully as his collar was taken off. In between the layers of leather, Tom took out the strip of window shade. He held it up, dangling. The letters of Buddy's cipher message stood out in the kitchen light.

"Oh, a cipher," said one of the new G men. "Can anybody read it?"

"Yes," said Mr. Godfrey. "It's the strip and stick cipher that Buddy and his chums worked out. Where is the stick?" he asked.

"Here," said Mrs. Martyne, producing a bit of curtain roller She had sensed the import of Gosum's return more quickly than any of the men. "Read it quickly!" she begged.

The strip of curtain from Buddy's prison

room was wound spirally about the stick. One end was marked with a short line. This was placed on the black line at the top of the stick. Harry held the stick while Tom wound the strip.

And when it was all wound, down to the very end, the cipher message stood out plainly:

IN TOWER HOUSE

"Hurray!" shouted Tom.

"Now we know where Buddy is!" cried Harry.

"This may mean something to you boys," said Mr. Godfrey, "but it is all Greek to me. What's the Tower House?"

Tom and Harry quickly explained, describing the location of the mansion of the eccentric astrologer and astronomer.

"Then if Buddy is there, so, very likely, is Mr. Weston," decided Mr. Godfrey. "We'll raid the place at once. Luckily we have sufficient men and we can get some extra police from here."

"But how can you be sure," asked one of the G men, "that this cipher message is from Buddy? Those spies know how to write and read ciphers."

"Look!" exclaimed Tom. "That's Buddy's secret signature." He pointed to a small, rough sketch of a pair of shoes and the figure 3 at the bottom of the strip. "Buddy can click his shoes together three times when he jumps up in the air," Tom explained.

"Then let's get going!" exclaimed Mr. Trainter. He took out his automatic and made sure it was in working order.

"May we come?" begged Tom and Harry together.

"No," said both their parents. But Mr. Godfrey said:

"Well, maybe you can look on at a distance—out of danger. I wish, though," he added, "we knew more about the layout of this Tower House. We're going at it sort of blind and in the dark. Usually, before we raid a hide-out, we diagram all the approaches and the lay of the surrounding country. We generally have a conference, and each man is assigned a certain approach. We'll have to go at this haphazard, I'm afraid. The spies may take alarm and skip."

"Wait a moment!" exclaimed Mr. Martyne. "I've just thought of something. Down the street is a real estate agent—Mr. Lang. He recently spoke to me about selling the old Tower House. He asked my help. He said he had been through it not so long ago and had a plan of it."

"Then he's the very man who can help us!" said Mr. Godfrey. "Get him here at once, please."

Mr. Lang, somewhat surprised to be called into the night conference, was soon at the Martyne home. He heard the story of the capture of Buddy and the G man.

"Yes, I have a rough plan of the house and the surrounding grounds," he said. "But if you want to get in there quietly, and surprise the gang, why not use the tunnel?"

"What tunnel?" asked Mr. Godfrey.

"Why, old Mr. Morrison, the astronomer, had an idea—a very foolish one—that, some day, he might want to escape in a hurry from his enemies. He really had no enemies except in his imagination. But he constructed a tunnel leading from the cellar out under the garden, several hundred feet. The outer end is beneath what appears to be a cold frame, for starting tomato and other plants in the Spring. Outwardly it looks like a cold frame of small glass panes. But when it is lifted you can go down a flight of steps and into the tunnel. I saw it when I made a plan of the house to use in advertising the place for sale. I don't know how this gang got in there."

"Well, we'll know how to get them out!" exclaimed Mr. Godfrey.

"Through the secret tunnel!" exclaimed Mr. Trainter.

"Let's go!" said one of the new G men.

CHAPTER XX

THE RESCUE

SOMEWHAT after midnight the rescue and raiding party of G men were ready to set out from Buddy's home to go to the Tower House.

After the cipher message had been read, and Mr. Lang had given information about the old mansion and the secret tunnel, the G men held a hasty conference.

On some pieces of grocery wrapping paper, which Lola Wagg supplied him, Mr. Godfrey drew a rough sketch of the house and the grounds, including the tunnel entrance. Each of the several G men was given a definite task to perform.

It wasn't known how many were in the gang holding captive Buddy and Mr. Weston.

"But I think we can handle them," said Mr. Godfrey, significantly.

So the raiding party started out under the

fitful light of a cloud-obscured moon. To their delight, Tom and Harry were allowed to accompany the G men, with Mr. Martyne as chaperon. He was told not to go beyond the tunnel entrance with Tom and Harry.

"But we would like to see that," Harry stipulated.

"We sure would," echoed his chum.

"Well, don't go beyond that, nor into the tunnel," warned Mr. Godfrey. "There may be shooting," he added.

"Golly! Wouldn't Buddy like to be there!" exclaimed Tom as the party started off, in several government cars, to the vicinity of Tower House.

"Be there!" said Harry. "Why, Buddy has a ringside seat!"

"That's right—he has," Tom admitted.

Much to his evident disgust, Gosum was left at home. They could take no chances on having him bark or whimper when he realized he was going back to Buddy. But Lola Wagg somewhat consoled the setter by giving him a bountiful, midnight meal. After which Gosum curled up and seemed to sleep.

But Mrs. Martyne, who remained up, noticed that the dog was ever on the alert, now and then opening an eye or cocking a listening ear. He wanted to know when Buddy came back.

"And I hope it will be soon," murmured Mrs. Martyne.

The raiding party parked the cars a short distance from the old mansion. The G man scouted around and reported the place to be in darkness and no evidence of guards being posted.

"I don't believe they suspect we know their hide-out," said Mr. Godfrey.

"Gosum got through their lines with the cipher message," said Tom.

"It's a good thing Buddy decided to go in for cipher mysteries," added Harry.

"There doesn't seem to be anything the

boys of today don't know," commented Mr. Martyne to the G men.

"That's right," agreed Mr. Godfrey. "Without Buddy's cipher message, we might have hunted for a week without discovering this Tower House hide-out."

Mr. Lang accompanied the raiders. He had recently made an examination of the premises, before the saboteurs picked it as one of their headquarters. He was able to lead the raiders straight to the secret tunnel entrance.

What appeared to be a hinged cold frame, built like a slanting cellar door, was raised. A flashlight revealed a flight of stone steps going down to a closed door.

"We may have to force that," said Mr. Godfrey. "It may make a noise and alarm the spies."

"The door isn't locked," said Mr. Lang. "I took the lock off the last time I was here. I don't believe those saboteurs know there is a tunnel opening into the cellar."

"Just where in the cellar does it come out?" asked Mr. Trainter.

"Behind another door, in front of which are a lot of old boxes and barrels. I moved them away but put them back again," said Mr. Lang. "The tunnel cellar door opens into the tunnel. You can get at the concealing boxes and barrels easily and move them aside without making any noise, I think."

"We'll make it a point to do so," said Mr. Godfrey. "We want to take these German saboteurs completely by surprise—before they get a chance to escape or harm Buddy or Mr. Weston. Now you boys stay here with Mr. Martyne," he added to Tom and Harry.

The two wanted very much to go down into the tunnel, but it would not have been wise nor safe. So they waited in the old garden, screened by trees and bushes, and hardly visible in the fitful moonlight.

At the appointed time, for each G man was taking note of the hour by his wrist watch, the raiders began closing in. They approached from several points outside the old mansion, and also through the tunnel.

As Mr. Lang had said, it was easy, once the underground passage was traversed, to move aside the boxes and barrels and enter the cellar. Up the inside cellar stairs went Mr. Godfrey and Mr. Trainter. They found the upper door bolted, but knew they could break this when the time came. Of course that would arouse the gang in the house. But by that time several outer doors would also be forced and the raid would be on in force.

At the top of the inside cellar stairs the two G men waited the signal from their comrades. This signal was to be one pistol shot, followed closely by two others. That would indicate the outer doors would be smashed in.

"I hope Weston is all right," whispered Mr. Trainter.

"So do I, and I hope Buddy is safe," added

Mr. Godfrey. "If we catch this gang, it will be much of Buddy's doing."

"That's right—his and Gosum's."

"Oh, yes, we mustn't forget the dog and the cipher."

They waited, silent in the darkness.

Suddenly a pistol shot rang out in the night. It was quickly followed by two more.

"Now!" cried Mr. Godfrey. He and Mr. Trainter put their shoulders to the cellar door and broke the bolt. They rushed into the kitchen, their flashlight glowing.

At the same moment there were crashing sounds at the back and front doors of the old house. The gang, suspecting nothing, had not barricaded the entrances.

"Surrender! We've got you surrounded!" shouted Mr. Godfrey.

The other G men shouted. They swarmed into the house, with drawn automatics and bright flashlights glowing.

There was a moment of silence following the surrender demands. Then, from upstairs, came the sound of running feet and a voice called:

"Who is it? What's the matter down there? Is that you Jule?" .

"We're G men. Come down with your hands in the air!" called Mr. Godfrey, standing at the foot of the front stairs. Mr. Trainter was at the back stairs. Other G men were at various intercepting points.

Silence upstairs followed the first confused inquiry. Then the crash of glass was heard and the thud of somebody landing outside the house in the bushes at the side of the mansion.

"One's got away," remarked a G man.

"He won't get far," commented Mr. Godfrey significantly.

The sound of a shot was heard, followed by a cry of pain and a voice whined:

"All right. Come and get me."

By this time several of the gang came down both stairways. Each member of the crowd of spies and saboteurs held his hands above his head. While some G men covered them with automatics, others snapped on handcuffs.

"Now then, are there any more of you?" demanded Mr. Godfrey.

"I guess you got us all," one of the gang sullenly said.

There was another thud on the ground, this time at the front of the house. Then came a second shot and a voice groaned:

"You got me, G man. I quit."

"That's Jule," said one of the captives.

"Shut up!" another warned. But it was too late.

"Now where's the boy and our other man?" sternly demanded Mr. Godfrey as the prisoners were herded into one room. No one answered for a moment and then Buddy's voice was heard yelling:

"Here I am! Is Gosum safe?"

"He sure is!' cried Mr. Trainter running toward the sound of Buddy's voice.

In a few more seconds Buddy was freed.

"Are Tom and Harry here?" he asked.

"At the tunnel entrance," said Mr. Godfrey.

"Is there a tunnel in this old place?" asked Buddy. "Hot dog! What a mystery!" He jumped up and clicked his heels three times.

"Do you know where Mr. Weston is, Buddy?" Mr. Godfrey asked.

"No, I haven't seen him since he was carried unconscious out of the boat."

"The G man is in an upstairs room," volunteered one of the captives. "He's all right, but a bit weak. Guess he'll need a doctor for the cut on his head."

Mr. Weston was soon found and released. He was painfully but not seriously hurt.

"I'm more mad than anything else that I let them get me," the G man complained to his comrades.

"Never mind," consoled Mr. Trainter. "It all happened for the best. I think we have the whole gang."

And so it proved. When the count was taken and the prisoners locked up, a big and important haul of German spies and saboteurs had been made. Much of the valuable electrical material was found hidden in the old house. There had not been time to get it away by motor boat, thanks to the chase by Mr. Weston and Buddy.

"Well," remarked Mr. Godfrey when the prisoners had been taken away, "I suppose you'd like to get back to your dog, Buddy?"

"Yes, where is he? Did he bring my cipher message?"

"He sure did! Without it we never would have been able to pull off tonight's raid," said Mr. Godfrey.

"Take me to Tom and Harry," begged Buddy.

And when the three chums were reunited

at the tunnel entrance, where Mr. Martyne waited, there was a joyful meeting.

"What'll you take for your dog, Buddy?" asked Mr. Godfrey when the G men, except those taking away the prisoners, were on their way back to Mouthchester.

"I wouldn't sell him for a million dollars!" Buddy exclaimed.

"I don't blame you," chuckled Mr. Trainter.

And when at home, a little later, Buddy threw his arms around Gosum's neck, it was difficult to tell which was the happier.

THE END